## Somewhere - a Sundown

When Blake Durant reached the town of Lincoln, he really should have just kept riding. But he didn't get the chance.

Within moments of his arrival, a gun-tough named Nico Semole injured his horse and then tried to pick a fight with an old man. Blake stopped him and beat him to pulp.

But Nico just didn't know when to quit. Later that day he came at Blake with a gun … and set off a chain of events that was to end in murder and bloody revenge.

Nico's brother Kent aimed to settle the account with Blake, and he had just enough gun-speed to do it. Furthermore, the local marshal was all burnt out, and Blake knew he couldn't rely on the man to keep the peace. So it looked as if the man they called The Loner would have to take matters into his own hands … and when he did, there was gunsmoke in the air and dead men on the ground.

We hope you enjoy this book. Please return or renew it by the due date.

You can renew it at www.norfolk.gov.uk/libraries or by using our free library app.

Otherwise you can phone 0344 800 8020 - please have your library card and PIN ready.

You can sign up for email reminders too.

NORFOLK ITEM

**30129 084 684 480**

NORFOLK COUNTY COUNCIL
LIBRARY AND INFORMATION SERVICE

# Somewhere - A Sundown

Sheldon B. Cole

A Black Horse Western

ROBERT HALE

First published by Cleveland Publishing Co. Pty Ltd,
New South Wales, Australia
First published in 1967
© 2020 Mike Stotter and David Whitehead

This edition © The Crowood Press, 2020
ISBN 978-0-7198-3128-7

The Crowood Press
The Stable Block
Crowood Lane
Ramsbury
Marlborough
Wiltshire SN8 2HR

www.bhwesterns.com

Robert Hale is an imprint
of The Crowood Press

Typeset by
Simon and Sons ITES Services Pvt Ltd
Printed and bound in Great Britain by
4Bind Ltd, Stevenage, SG1 2XT

# ONE

## LINCOLN

Blake Durant took a firmer hold on his blue-black stallion, Sundown, as far-off thunder muttered among the peaks of the mountains he had just traveled through. Below him the country leveled out into lush, green prairie where a large herd of winter-fattened cattle grazed leisurely. It was by far the best country he'd seen in a year of drifting. As he rode down from the craggy heights the muttering of thunder continued among the cliffs and boulders, sounding like a disgruntled man in his sleep. Durant felt good. He'd taken his time after riding out of Lusc, had even done some fishing and hunting. Now he was on the way to Lincoln.

The wind, no more than a light breeze against his back, had the smell of rain in it. In the lower country the silence folded about him. It was the kind of day that made a man thoughtful. He thought of Lusc and his trouble there. A man had died under the fury of his gun, but he'd deserved no better than death and nobody lamented his passing. However, the memory of the gunfight remained fixed in Blake Durant's mind, mixed with other memories, of a woman he had loved but who, like the trouble-maker in Lusc, was now dead. Dust and distance were now all that mattered to him. His trails led to nowhere in particular, going on and on, bringing him into conflict with men who disliked him for no particular reason, who misunderstood him ... men who could never leave well enough alone.

Durant rubbed the neck of the big stallion and moved steadily towards his destination. He knew little about Lincoln, but he'd been told it was a prosperous community where work was generally available to a man not frightened to sweat. With work a man could blank his mind. Durant needed to do that, needed to keep himself occupied in the present so as to blot out the searing pain of the past. He rounded a bend in the trail and then Lincoln was just beneath him.

It was a bigger town than he'd expected, with two main streets. Four narrow streets cut into the two main streets, forming fifteen sections of almost equal size. It was late afternoon, still a couple of hours till sundown, and the people were out in force. It might have been election day in Lusc or the day after roundup in Cheyenne.

Ten minutes later he rode into the main street, a big man, tall in the saddle, relaxed, expecting nothing more from this town than he was willing to put into it. His hide coat flapped against his tight-muscled body and a golden bandanna covered his neck. On his hip was a Colt .45 in a worn holster. His stallion's hide gleamed brightly as he stepped out with effortless grace, the horse eyeing the people on the boardwalk who showed no interest at all.

There were indeed plenty of people on the street, cowhands in the careless garb of the rangeland, well-dressed ranchers and businessmen, gamblers in the sober black of their trade, prospectors with their battered hats shading eyes that still had dreams in them. Women, too, old and young; the old suspicious, the younger ones taking Durant in with undisguised admiration. Before he had gone fifty yards into the town Blake Durant decided he liked it. There was an air of excitement here that appealed to him.

Things were happening and promised to go on happening. It was a town big enough to get lost in.

Blake Durant worked Sundown close to the overhang of the buildings. He saw one saloon and ignored it, then he passed an eatery and a line of business houses. The street began to broaden out, showing the bulk of the town before him. People were coming and going, some hurrying, some taking their time. Horses were hitched to the street racks, and a freighter bounced along, its wheels lifting dust which after the rain would become mud.

Blake Durant sighted a low-ceilinged building. A sign creaking on iron hooks proclaimed it to be the sheriff's office. Blake turned Sundown towards the place, noting that a second saloon, bigger and more gaily painted than the first, stood a short distance away, beside the biggest building in the street, Cattlemen's Rest.

Blake was walking Sundown to the hitch rail when a tall, swarthy young man smoking a short cigar, stepped from the saloon laneway. His glance flicked at Durant and went over Sundown. Immediate admiration for the big horse showed in his coal black eyes. His gaze lifted again and his lips curled back sneeringly. At that moment, Blake saw the conceit and meanness of many of his kind, half-breeds who wanted no part of whites or Mexicans. They were outcasts by choice, men who lived in a world of their own bitterness.

Durant came a little taller in the saddle. The faraway look in his eyes was gone. He sat there, tensed for action like a set trap. The swarthy man took one step towards him, eyes still running over Sundown covetously. He seemed about to speak to Blake when something caught his attention across the street and behind Durant.

The tall man was grinning and his eyes were agleam with excitement. Then he looked about him before breaking into a run up the boardwalk. Blake turned Sundown around and saw the tall man sprint past the jailhouse wall and then along the boardwalk to the street corner where a buckboard stood. An old man was trying to climb to the buckboard seat. The tall man grabbed the old-timer by the shirt-front and yanked him down so hard that he fell to the street on the seat of his pants. Then the half-breed leaped into the driving seat and grabbed up the reins.

Blake moved Sundown slightly out from the boardwalk. This was none of his business, but he couldn't let himself stand by and see the old man so roughly handled. Then the buckboard was coming fast, straight for Blake. He jerked the big horse's head up and had a quick look around before he kicked Sundown into a run. The buckboard came on, with the dark-skinned youth slashing a whip across the backs of the two terrified horses.

For a moment Blake thought he might avoid the collision but then Sundown faltered and the swinging rear of the buckboard clipped him on his left foreleg. Sundown let out a nicker of pain and fear and buckled over, sending Durant out of the saddle. He landed in the street and rolled. Looking up, he saw the youth turn on the seat and leer at him.

Then the buckboard went on. Sundown had hit the ground on his side but had fought his way upright immediately. Now he stood there, his sides quivering. Blake pulled him close and quietened him, then he examined the horse's foreleg. A streak of blood ran down the black glossy hide.

"It's all right, boy," Blake said soothingly.

The buckboard had turned around up the street and was coming back, the youth still belting the horse furiously. Blake led Sundown towards the jailhouse boardwalk where the dazed old-timer was slowly dragging himself to his feet. Blake thrust the reins into his gnarled hands and said, "Watch him for me. His leg's hurt, so he'll give you no trouble."

He went up the street before the dazed old man could answer him. Long strides took him quickly to the other side of the street where a young woman stood on the boardwalk, her face white with fear. As the buckboard closed in on her she gave a sharp cry and began to run. The dark-skinned young man reined the buckboard to a halt, leaped to the ground and made after her.

Durant sprinted after the two of them. Soon the woman turned into a cottage yard before the dark-skinned youth reached the gate. He made a move to go up the pathway when a voice barked:

"Far enough, Semole! Come one more step and I'll blow your stinkin' guts out!"

Blake slowed, watching the youth's hand slide towards his gun. The glitter of excitement had left the dark man's eyes and was replaced by a dull, flat angry look. His lips curled back in a sneer.

"Don't push your luck, boy!" the voice went on.

Blake, moving past the last storefront, saw a stoop shouldered old man standing on the cottage porch. He held an old rifle that was leveled at the youth.

"You callin' me, Graham?" the youth demanded to know. "You buttin' into my business?"

"My granddaughter is my business, boy," the white-haired old man said.

11

Not a hint of fear showed in his weathered old face and his hands were as steady as rock. Tall and slight, he looked anything but a match for this powerfully proportioned youth, but Blake knew he would see this business through.

Blake was only ten yards from Semole now. The young woman had gone up the steps and was looking fearfully at the scene from the front doorway. There was no sound in the street. Semole still had his hand clapped on his gun butt.

Then Blake saw the curl of the young half-breed's fingers, saw the forearm muscles go taut. He hurried his last steps to Semole, grasped his gun arm and pulled him about.

Semole, whose full attention had been given to the old man, grunted in surprise. Then he said:

"Don't buy in, stranger."

Blake shook his head. "You ran down my horse and might have hurt him badly, mister. I don't let anybody get away with that."

Semole's eyes flashed angrily. He broke from Blake's grip and took a step back. Then his lips curled viciously again.

"You don't let anybody!" he snapped. "Now who the hell do you think you are? By hell—"

Semole lunged, driving out a left for Blake's face. Blake ducked the punch and ripped a right into Semole's stomach. Then he swung a back-hand which sent Semole crashing into the fence, shaking it along its full length.

Hurt and surprised, Semole pushed himself from the fence, wiped a hand across his mouth and looked at the blood on it. Then he glared at Durant and swung up his gun. Blake moved into him and drove his wrist down and onto a fence paling. A sharp cry came from Semole as the gun spun from his grip and fell into the yard. Blake grabbed the man's shoulder and hurled him away. When Semole went sprawling to the ground, he said:

"I don't let a gun brat take on a young woman and an old man either, Semole. Now get to hell out of here before I remember you might have crippled my horse for good."

Semole sat on the seat of his pants, wild fury contorting his face. "You're in, mister, and I'm not letting you out."

Blake stood spraddle-legged and waited for Semole to get to his feet. The half-breed wiped a hand across his mouth again and then he looked about for his gun. Unable to find it, he straightened, deep hatred in his dark face. He moved a little to the right, then swayed back to the left, his shrewd eyes sizing up this stranger. What he saw must have made him decide to be cautious

13

because he stayed back, drawing in deep gulps of air. He glanced at the old man and then his gaze sought out the young woman. A grin split his mouth and he nodded twice before giving a grunt of satisfaction.

"Okay, big man, now we'll see. You might not know it, but you just bought yourself more trouble than you've ever stepped on in your life. I'm gonna tear you apart."

"I'm waiting," Durant said. But then came the voice of the old man:

"Best leave it as it stands, stranger. I got a bead on him. If he don't shift off and leave us alone, I'll send a blast into him that'll put him where he belongs."

Blake's stare didn't leave Semole's dark eyes. Across the street people were gathering, but no one came forward to interfere. That, and Semole's utter confidence in himself, told Blake a great deal.

Then Semole came at him, fast, furious, a big man throwing punches packed with terrific power. Blake went back under the heavy onslaught and Semole followed him, grinning widely, clearly enjoying the taste of success.

For half a minute Semole's attack was aimed at Blake's head, but then, swiftly and cunningly, he sent his punches to the body. Blake felt the full power of two rips into his stomach before he could dodge aside. Realizing now that he had a king-sized fight on his hands, he waded in. His fists belted out a vicious tattoo on Semole's head and face, sending him back and making him raise his hands in defense. One of Blake's punches opened his right eyebrow and another smashed his nose. Blood spurted and Semole's legs began to wobble. But somehow he stayed up.

Blake kept at him. Systematically he cut down the big man's strength until he had him gasping for breath and whistling through his teeth. But Semole would not give in. The speed was gone from his legs and his punches weren't nearly as powerful, but he managed to jump back from a heavy blow that would have ended the fight. He bounced off the fence and clutched at Blake. Getting a hold, he hung on. Blake drove his hands up between their chests and heaved him away, then he hit him with a blow that split his right cheek open and sent him tottering to the side.

"Go all the way, stranger," called the old man on the porch. The old warrior's eyes were gleaming with excitement. He had lowered the gun and was resting on it, using it as a prop. "You let his kind up, boy, and you got all hell to deal with.

Finish him good—cut him right down to snake-belly size."

Blake had no wish to do this. In his opinion Semole had fought bravely and he admired him for it, even if he was in the wrong and likely always had been. He was a bully, an overbearing, high-stepping, rough-riding bully, but he was certainly no coward.

Now Semole glared up at him, black eyes staring from his bloody face. He was breathing heavily, air wheezing through his tortured lungs and smashed nose.

Blake said, "I'm willing to call it quits, Semole."

Semole straightened and hate blasted from his black eyes. He wiped his face with his sleeve, leaving it as blood-smeared as his features. Blood poured unchecked from the cheek gash.

"Give yourself a name," Semole grated out.

"Blake Durant," Blake said, hoping Semole would see the sense in quitting.

"Durant." Semole said the name as if putting it in his memory for later reference. Then he said, "Durant, you're a dead man."

"I don't think so, Semole. You asked for all you got. Why not leave it at that?"

Semole's lips twisted and he steadied himself against the fence. A paling came loose in his hand and suddenly his eyes brightened. He stepped away and pulled the paling free. Going into a crouch, he began to circle Durant. Blake moved away from him until he found himself pinned against the fence. A nail in the heavy paling glittered.

The old man cried out, "You're a low-bellied scum, Semole. Take your beating like a man."

Semole said, "I'm takin' him and then you, Graham. Then the girl. She's done her last bit of struttin' in the street and spittin' in my face. Ain't nobody, and especially not this driftin' cowpoke, gonna stop me from takin' her."

Semole was leering again, his strength returning with the feel of the paling in his hands. He held it near his knee, horizontal to the ground, and then he lunged, swinging. Blake went under the timber, but Semole stopped the swing suddenly and brought the paling back viciously. The nail came within an inch of Blake's face.

Blake waited, feet loosely planted, his body braced to go in any direction. Semole came in again, swinging wildly, annoyed by his first failure. Blake backed off, dodged, weaved under the timber until he'd maneuvered Semole against the fence. Then he hurled himself onto the man. The paling came up and smashed across the side of his head. He felt a drive of pain go down the back of his head and into his neck. But he had the 'breed in a headlock with his left arm. His right fist went back and he pistoned it into Semole's face. A cry of pain came from Semole. Blake held the headlock and smashed all the fight out of the 'breed with his right hand before hurling him to the ground. Semole struggled to a kneeling position, gave a groan and then fell onto his side.

Blake brought a hand to his neck. He felt the stickiness of blood. Pain lanced through his head and down his back.

The old man was coming down the steps now. His face was awash with admiration and excitement. "Hell, boy, you did him in real good. Too damn good maybe." He stopped and inspected Semole, then nudged him in the ribs with the barrel of his gun. He chuckled when Semole didn't respond to the prod. Then the old man's face went grave again.

"You'd best head out though, stranger. Semole's bad clean through. He won't take a beating like this and let it go at that, no sir. He'll get his strength back and then he'll come for you again. Next time it'll be guns and there ain't nobody can match him in that kind of fight, at least nobody I ever saw."

The old-timer put out his hand. "Hardy Graham. The young woman is my granddaughter, Joy. Semole's been givin' her a lot of trouble

18

of late but until now we didn't figure even he would go this far. My son's the sheriff, so I'll see him and get this scum thrown out of town. You go on your way though mister. Be better for you."

Blake looked past him towards the house. He saw the frightened face of the young woman behind the side window. It seemed to him that she was looking straight at him, but sunlight against the window made it impossible for him to be sure.

"I've got a horse to see to," Blake told Hardy Graham.

"Then do that and then ride out, mister. No good will come of staying and lockin' horns with this crazy killer. One way or another he'll try to get even with you. He's a sneak, but he's cunnin' and, like I said, he's bad, clear through. For what you did, I'm obliged, real obliged. You remind me of myself, as I was, before a couple too many years got piled on my head."

Blake gave Semole another brief look before he turned and went on his way. Halfway down the street he stopped to duck his head into a water trough. He came up spluttering, then splashed water over his face and neck. He felt only a slight sting of pain in his neck and when he worked his shoulders he found his muscles to be free enough. Crossing the street, he noticed that a big crowd had gathered outside the saloon and more people were lined along the boardwalk down from them. But nobody approached him.

Reaching the old-timer Semole had first mauled, Blake took Sundown's reins from him. The old-timer studied him heavily for a moment before he said:

"Leg's bruised, no more."

"That's how I figured it," Blake said.

"Be a day or two before he can stride out, though." Blake read the concern behind the words and led Sundown off. But the old-timer followed along the boardwalk and said, "You want a horse to ride out on? I can give you one and I'll look after this feller for you till you come back."

Blake turned into the livery stable laneway. "I'll leave when I'm good and ready," he said and went on his way.

The old-timer drew his bony body to full height and nodded. His colorless old eyes were thoughtful as he muttered: "Yeah, boy, you'd do that. You'd do that and tell them all to kiss the seat of your pants. Pity. Good men don't deserve to die."

Blake Durant didn't hear him. He continued on his way and found that the stable attendant was another old man, whose hands when they

20

shifted over Sundown's injured leg, brought no complaint from the horse.

"Good 'un, this feller," he said. "By hell, I ain't seen many better. Be proud to have him in my place, stranger, for as long as you feel he should stay."

"Two days should see him fit again," Blake said. "That's your opinion."

"About."

Blake went off, feeling the old man's curious eyes taking him in. He strode along the board-walk, working his shoulders and neck against the lingering pain. His fists were swollen and bruised and his ribs hurt when he dragged in a deep breath.

Lincoln, a town where work was plentiful. He smiled to himself. Lincoln was just another name in a long list of towns that meant trouble for Blake Durant. He turned into the saloon watched by half the townspeople.

A short distance away, Nico Semole, under the leveled gun of Hardy Graham, dragged himself into a back street to lick his wounds.

And to plot …

# TWO

## "DURANT!"

The barkeep was a grizzly of a man with big, iron-knuckled hands and skin that looked like stretched rawhide. He seemed so out of place behind his counter, an apron on his waist, that Blake Durant had to look around to make sure he was in the right place.

The big man's face split into a wide, friendly grin. "Guess you want a drink, eh, stranger? Two maybe, or a full damn bottle. For you, the best— private stock and at the right price and to hell with the hangover that might come after."

The barkeep placed a bottle of unlabelled whisky on the counter and took his money from Blake's scattered change. Nobody in the saloon had tried to approach Durant. Lincoln people

22

were obviously wary of him. Or maybe they didn't want to be linked with him.

"What about this feller, Semole?" he said to the barkeep. "Top gun?"

The barkeep's warmth dissolved and his eyes narrowed thoughtfully. After a moment he nodded his head. "He's good, real damn good. And he'll come after you, no mistake about that. You got your bottle, so why not go outside and drink in the quiet? Better still, get on your horse and drink as you ride."

Blake filled his glass again. "Seems to me to be a quiet enough place here."

The barkeep grinned crookedly. "I'm not worryin' about me or my place, mister. But you beat up Nico Semole real good. Around here that puts a man on the Boothill trail."

Blake emptied his glass. The barkeep filled it for him this time, then mopped up a small pool of rye a short way down the counter. When the huge man began to serve other customers, Blake leaned over the counter and stared moodily into his drink. Why move on? he asked himself. Why run just because a gun brat had stepped out of line and had been put in his place? Yet a lingering worry stayed in his mind, held there by the fact that everybody here was concerned about Semole's next move. Despite the fight, Blake carried no great dislike for the wild-tempered Nico Semole. The half-breed had shown great courage. Blake just hoped that Semole had some friends who would talk him out of taking the matter further.

Blake was halfway through his third drink and beginning to unwind when a man bumped his left shoulder. Blake turned and moved just enough to give his right hand room for free movement. He looked into a long, tight-skinned face. The man had a trim moustache over his pinched mouth and his hands were spread loosely on the counter. He was making it clear that he wanted no trouble. Blake held the newcomer's stare evenly. The man had a tin star on his checked shirt and he wore a single gun.

The small mouth opened. "I'm Sheriff Alec Graham."

"I've already met your father," Blake said.

"Yeah. Pa told me, Durant. He also told me the rest of it—how Semole near killed your horse after manhandling my jailer, and how he chased my daughter up the boardwalk. Pa said you bought in and took over from him, saved him from having to kill Semole."

"It might not have come to that," Blake said easily and sipped his drink, still studying Alec Graham over the rim of his glass. The men in the room had ceased to chatter and the barkeep, mopping his counter, had his head cocked in a listening attitude some ten feet away.

"Might not have come to shooting, and then again it might have, Durant," said Alec Graham. He removed his Stetson and ran a hand through his thinning hair. Blake put him down at over forty years of age, maybe closing on fifty. By the look of him, he either worked too hard or worried a lot. Probably the latter, he decided.

"As far as I'm concerned it's finished now," Blake put in after a moment.

Graham licked his lips and shook his head. A knot of worry appeared in his thin, high forehead.

"It's far from finished, I'm afraid, Durant. Nico Semole is rotten clear through. He won't take a beating and just leave it at that, not him."

"So everybody tells me," Blake said casually and spent some time filling his glass. "Free to drink now, Sheriff?"

Graham looked at the whisky bottle and shook his head. "Never drink before sundown and only a little then, Durant. Thanks all the same. After pa told me what happened, I figured I'd seek you out and help you all I can. The best advice I can give you is this—saddle up and ride. Ole, my jailer, said your horse isn't hurt bad and could be nursed along the trail."

"I just got here," Blake Durant said quietly.

Graham frowned deeply and straightened, slipping his hands off the counter and wiping them down his shirt front. "You don't seem to understand. I'm not telling you to run and hide. I'm just asking you to be sensible, for both our sakes."

"Does Semole worry you, Sheriff?" Blake pushed at him and saw the frown go deeper in the lined brow.

"Maybe, Durant," Graham admitted. "That doesn't make me no coward, if that's what you mean to imply. The way I see the position, it makes me damned sensible. Nico Semole is the fastest gun in these parts. He's already killed half a dozen men to my knowledge and maybe another half dozen he's not been made to answer for. Add to that the fact that he's mean enough to tear anybody down—any way he can—and you should get some idea of what you're up against if you stay."

Blake wiped his mouth on the back of his hand. His gaze swung past Alec Graham to take in the customers. He noticed that some looked worried, some were just plain curious, and others had an air of expectancy about them.

Blake said, "When I rode in, Graham, I figured this was a nice, homely little town that just might have something for me in it. Nothing that's happened since has given me any cause to change that opinion. As for Semole … well, most towns have a hard case or two like him. So I'll stay and give my horse plenty of time to get fit. Meantime I'll have some drinks. When I'm ready to go I'll push on, not before."

"Don't be so damned stubborn!" snapped Graham—louder than he meant to, Blake figured, because the lawman looked anxiously about him after speaking. Then Graham wiped sweat from his brow and lowered his voice. "Look, Durant, this isn't your town. If it comes right down to the point, Nico Semole has more right here than you do. You're the stranger, you're the intruder."

A rise of annoyance lifted in Durant. "Do you give a man like Semole special rights in your town, Sheriff? Maybe there are a couple of things you should think about. He chased a young woman with the intention of mauling her. He would have drawn against your father if the old man hadn't beaten him to it with his rifle. And from what I've been told by you and your townsmen, Semole has been riding roughshod over everybody, doing as he damn well pleases. What the hell kind of reasoning are you using, Sheriff?"

The color drained from Alec Graham's face and he licked at his lips. He was quiet for a long moment before he said, in a strained voice that Blake could barely hear, "I'm telling you, Durant, you don't know the man. You beat him in a fist brawl, but when it comes to a gun he's another man entirely. I tell you, he can't be beat."

Blake freshened his drink. "Sheriff, I think you've told me enough for now. Whatever else you have to say won't interest me."

Blake turned to leave and Alec Graham grasped his arm. "What is it?" Blake asked coldly. "Maybe you've got ideas about riding me out of town on a rail?"

"Don't be a damned fool, Durant. I'm obliged for what you did for pa and I can tell you that you've got the respect of more than just me in this town. It's a good town and maybe someday it'll be the kind of place that's got what you're looking for. But not now. Ride out and do us both a favor, you and me. I swear to you that it's for the best."

Blake shrugged out of the sheriff's grip and walked away without a word. He heard Alec Graham curse under his breath, then he heard the sheriff's boots pound along the boards towards the front of the saloon. He pulled a chair up to a table where two cowhands were sitting. The two men exchanged a quick look and rose together.

"Time we were pulling out, Jude," one muttered. Then giving Durant a nod, both made their way back to the bar counter.

Blake poured himself another drink and swirled it about in the glass. There was a rumble of talk in the room now, but he could make nothing of importance out of it.

Everyone thought Nico Semole would come after him in time. Well, if that happened, so be it. But he didn't intend to make a shooting match out of his argument with Semole. He'd talk, put Semole right on a couple of matters, and let it go at that. If further trouble came it would be Semole's doing.

Half an hour went by before the talk, which had grown louder in the saloon, suddenly stopped. In the silence that followed, Blake heard the back door close. Then footsteps came towards him. He didn't bother to turn.

"Durant!"

The voice had venom in it. Blake turned slowly in his chair, pulling his glass across the table with the movement. His stare lifted and took in the bruised face of Nico Semole.

"Do you want something?" Blake asked casually.

"Yeah, Durant—I want you. Up, mister, and no talk. I'm here to kill you."

Blake shook his head slowly. "Nobody's going to kill me, Semole."

"Up, damn you, or take it cold where you sit!"

Semole's hand was clamped on his gun butt. Blake slowly came to his feet, then coolly finished his drink. He put the glass down and held Semole's fierce, hate-filled gaze.

"Our trouble is finished with, Semole. You stepped out of line and I hammered you for it. Let's leave it at that."

"Show me how you can use that big gun of yours, Durant," Semole said tightly. "See if you can shoot before I put a slug in you and blast your interferin' guts all over this room."

The crowd backed off, giving Semole and Blake the middle of the room. Behind Semole a lantern burned on a high shelf. The back door was open and the gloom of evening filled the yard. There was no sound at all.

Blake spread his feet wide and said, "Semole, you'll be making a bad mistake."

"Draw, damn you!"

Semole's hand jerked down suddenly and Blake realized he'd let the 'breed get the jump on him. His own hand flashed down, took hold and lifted the gun clear of leather. His action was fast and smooth. He pumped off one shot that slammed into Nico Semole's left shoulder and sent him spinning away. A runt of a man in cowhand garb let out a shout as Semole's body crashed against him. With the smell of cordite in his nostrils, Blake stood ready for Semole's next move.

The half-breed regained his balance, hurled the small cowboy aside and wheeled about, hate flashing in his eyes.

Durant said, "I warned you."

But Semole paid the advice no heed. His gun lifted and Blake punched off his second shot and the bullet slammed with a dull thud into the 'breed's chest. Semole went back on his heels, his face drained of color. Horror flooded into his face, then surprise washed away terror and his legs gave way.

"No!" he breathed as he hit the floor on his face. His gun slithered across the floor to disappear under a table. Blake's smoking gun stayed on target, but Nico Semole didn't move. Nor did another sound come from him.


"By hell and tarnation, you done it, Durant!"

Hardy Graham came pounding into the room as the echo of the last shot died. He brushed three townsmen aside and stood grinning down at the body of Nico Semole. "Took him fair and square with about the fastest damn draw I ever seen in my life. And I seen plenty in my day. Seen the best of them. The Kromer boys, Luke Short, Pete Madder. Weren't nobody to hold a candle to them when it came to a shootout. But, by hell, Durant, what you just done and how you done it, hardly even blinkin' an eye—well, I reckon it deserves mention with the best of all the gunfights. For the second time today, mister, I'm gonna shake your hand."

Before Blake could move his hand was being pumped vigorously. He pulled his hand away finally and moved back from the grinning, excited old man. Hardy Graham left him and pushed his way through a knot of men to the bar counter. He thumped his hands on the counter and called out:

"Hap, set 'em up all around—and you're payin', by hell!"

Hap Tonkin straightened behind his counter, surprise lifting his heavy brows.

"Do it for Durant, Hap, for him getting rid of your biggest trouble maker, Nico Semole," Hardy Graham insisted. "Durant just gave this town the biggest boost it's had in ten years. With Semole out of the way it means the rest of us can breathe more freely. Now the sheriff don't have to worry about waitin' for Semole to make a big mistake. And everybody here—yeah, every single one of you men who've been made shift ground when Nico Semole came stompin' in—all of you can relax. So how about it, Hap?"

Hap Tonkin frowned heavily and spent time counting off the number of men present. Most of the customers had already hurried across to the counter to take up their positions.

"Yeah, Hap, what about it? Semole's been givin' you hell and you owe Durant plenty for what he's done."

A tall townsman moved alongside Hardy Graham, grinning. Then others began to shout, giving further backing to the suggestion. Finally, Hap Tonkin, sucking in a loud breath, held his hands up for quiet and announced:

"Okay, okay, everybody quiet down. I had it in mind to set drinks up for all anyway. But first let's get Blake Durant up here. And don't nobody touch Semole. Leave him be till Alec gets here and is told how it happened. Quiet now and no pushin'. There's plenty of booze to go around."

A loud chorus of cheering broke out and the rush forward was enough to rock the counter. Tonkin lifted full bottles from under his counter and handed them out.

Blake holstered his gun and watched the melee of shuffling, excited men. He was soon left on his own, standing against the table looking down at the bloodied body of Nico Semole, a man he hardly knew, a man like so many other fools he'd met.

"Okay, okay, quiet now."

Sheriff Alec Graham pushed himself through the crowd of drinkers and pulled his father away from the counter, all the while studying Blake Durant curiously. The lawman seemed in no way worried. In fact, Blake thought he looked relieved about the night's business.

While Blake waited for the lawman to come across and question him, Hardy Graham and Hap Tonkin gave their accounts of the shooting. Alec Graham heard them out, then left his father and came slowly across the room. He bit on his bottom lip and seemed to be trying to look serious, but there was a gleam of excitement in his eyes while a smile struggled to break out on his thin lips.

"Guess you don't have to answer to anybody for the killing, Durant," he said, drawing up to Blake. "Everybody knows it was a fair fight and Semole did the calling. In a way I'm obliged, which I guess you can understand."

Blake looked blandly at him and poured himself a drink. Finally he said, "What do we do with Semole, Sheriff—leave him there?"

Alec Graham's gaze moved across the floor to the body. Pulling his gunbelt tighter about his lean waist, he replied gruffly, "Hell, no. What do you take me for, Durant? I'll see him buried, sure enough, good riddance or not."

"Then the sooner he's taken from here the better, isn't it?" Blake pushed.

Graham's lips thinned and an angry gleam came into his eyes. "Now hold on Durant. Just because you took care of him and have proved yourself one hell of a fast gun, it doesn't give you the right to—"

"Nothing gives anybody rights they don't deserve, Sheriff," Blake said quietly. "I'm not riding high. Fact of the matter is, I'm damned disgusted about the way things went. Maybe if some of you people had taken a stand in the past, Semole wouldn't have walked into this thinking he could beat the whole world. Bury him well, at least he had the guts to keep coming."

Blake picked up his bottle and moved away from the tight-featured lawman. He hesitated halfway across the room, feeling the eyes of the whole crowd following him. For a brief moment he thought of the home he had left and of people he had known who were no longer sharply defined in his mind. He felt a sudden sadness take hold of him and he wondered if anything was worth a damn any longer.

Moving slowly on, he looked into the yard where night had fully closed in. A cool wind came through the doorway. Then, giving the body of Nico Semole one last glance, he walked towards the yard.

"Damn him, he figures me for a coward," growled Alec Graham. "He reckons I should have tamed Semole before this—should have taken him by the scruff of the neck and pitched him out of town."

Hap Tonkin, old Hardy Graham and a knot of townsmen heard the lawman out without comment. Some of the drinkers had gone home, but a considerable crowd remained, talking about the street brawl and the gunfight and the killing of Nico Semole. The fact that Durant meant to stay in town didn't matter to them, now. He'd left his mark, and in doing so had shown he was anything but a bloodthirsty hellion. He had given the impression that he was a loner, an unapproachable man, a drifter without ties and with no real wish to have any. Much speculation was voiced about him. Who was he? Where had he come from? How did he get to be so fast with a gun without his reputation spreading through-out the frontier?

As the crowd talked, Hardy Graham led his son along the bar. Standing tall, his grey hair slicked down on his big head, he placed a fatherly hand on the lawman's shoulder, and said, "You haven't lived as I have and learned how to understand Durant's kind, son. I know his breed—I rubbed shoulders with 'em during the war and along the Platte later on. I've seen his kind, twisted inside by doubts about them-selves and driftin' around, lookin' for somethin' they can't give a name to. Nobody blames you for not handling Nico Semole, boy, and nobody ever will. Semole was a cur, sure, but Durant now ... listen, son, no matter how fair he's acted since coming here, make sure he watches his manners. I wouldn't take much from him. In fact, if I was the man wearing the badge, I'd have me a hard talk with Durant and put him in his place. Semole was good with a gun, sure. But how damned good? Who did he ever cut down who really mattered? A few drunken cowboys, no more. For mine, Durant hasn't proved him-self so damned great we should let him walk tall, all over us. We're obliged, my family more than anybody, I guess, but that obligation shouldn't be allowed to blind us to the truth that Blake Durant is no better than any gunfighter. We'll tolerate him for only as long as he keeps the peace from now on."

Alec Graham looked heavily at his father and wiped sweat from his brow. Then Hap Tonkin revealed his presence by muttering under his breath. Old Hardy Graham glared at the barkeep.

"You differ on that, Hap?" the old warrior asked sharply.

Tonkin shrugged, then grinned crookedly. "Seems to me that folks change their minds right quick in this town. This morning we were all walkin' the opposite side of the street to Nico Semole, wonderin' when his brother would be back and them two would run riot again. But now, just as soon as that weight is lifted off us, we start to sprout up out of our boots."

"Sprout?" Hardy Graham echoed. "What the hell are you talkin' about, Tonkin? I've always been the same height, as tall as my past gives me the right to be. By hell, if I was your age I'd have shown Semole something. And Durant, too, if he came around lookin' for trouble."

The townsmen began to shift off, leaving Hardy Graham glaring after them.

Alec straightened the tin star on his shirt and said quietly, "Well, who's gonna help bury Semole? Best get it done right away."

Neither Tonkin nor Hardy Graham offered to help. Scowling, Alec Graham finished his drink and moved towards Semole's body. He stopped and looked down before glancing about the saloon for assistance. But even in death it seemed that Nico Semole was a loner in this town.

Alec Graham snapped, "Some of you boys get there and give me a hand. He can't bite you now."

As he spoke a slim brunette burst into the saloon from the back yard. She looked anxiously about her for some time. When the townsmen drew back, she asked, "Where is my brother? Where is Nico?"

She turned her fierce gaze onto Hap Tonkin and the barkeep pointed to where Sheriff Graham stood. "There he is, Therese. There's your brother."

Therese Semole followed the direction of Tonkin's gaze. When she saw her brother sprawled on the floor she let out a cry and ran across the room. The lawman was too slow in getting out of her way, so she shoved him roughly aside and dropped down, already sobbing, at Nico's side. No one in the room spoke.

The girl hugged her brother's face against her bosom, rocking back and forth and crying. After a while she lowered his head to the floor gently and glared up at Graham.

"Who did it?"

"Man name of Durant. A newcomer, Miss Semole. It was a fair fight."

"You liar!" Therese cried. She jumped to her feet and began striking at the retreating Graham, hitting his neck and shoulders with her fists. "Liar! Nobody in this town could kill my brother unless he resorted to murder. What happened? Who was here?"

Graham pushed her away and swore under his breath. Then he said, "The saloon was full and everybody who counts in town saw it plain, damn you! Your brother bit off more than he could chew this time. He made a call and got killed for his trouble."

Therese made to punch at him again and he backed off. Then she spun about, her dark eyes flashing at the men lined along the counter. "Tell me the truth!" she demanded. "I want to know!"

"The sheriff had it right," Tonkin said. "Man name of Blake Durant rode in and locked horns with Nico. Durant beat the stuffin' outa Nico as you can see by his face. Nico didn't leave it at that and came after him with his gun. He didn't make it, and that's the truth."

Therese Semole walked slowly towards the bar, nostrils dilated, eyes wild. Men stepped out of her way, clearly wanting no part of her. But Hardy Graham stood defiantly in her path.

"That is the God's truth, young woman," he told her firmly. "And it's about time, I say. Now maybe you and the rest of your kind will leave this town alone."

Therese gave a sharp little cry and slapped the old man's face. "You're the biggest liar of them all! You've never said a true word in all your life! Yes, I've heard the stupid stories of how great a man you were. Your son is no better—he is a coward, not fit to polish Nico's boots. As for your prim and proper daughter—she is a lie herself with all her sweet smiles. *You* and your whole family leave a stink behind you when you walk in the streets, old man!"

Hardy Graham's face paled and his hands twisted at his belt buckle. But before he could get any words out, Therese pushed him away disdainfully and confronted the perspiring Hap Tonkin again.

"You said his name is Blake Durant, Tonkin?"

Tonkin nodded.

"Where is he hiding? Has he saddled up and left? If he has, I tell you now that Kane will hunt him down and kill him."

Tonkin shook his head. "Last I seen of him he went into the yard, keepin' to himself. Hell, now don't you start on us. We didn't have anything to do with it. It was Nico and Durant and nobody else was involved."

Therese leaned forward and spat in his face. "Scum and liar!" she screamed and then she wheeled about, lashing out at a few men who hadn't withdrawn far enough. "All of you hated Nico. You were frightened of him!" Sending them scattering, Therese Semole strode down the room, pulling her shawl tight across her slender shoulders. A deep-seated hate rode her eyes and her lips were curled back into a snarl of vicious rage. She hadn't reached the back door when Blake Durant stepped into sight. Therese stopped dead in her tracks and her features became taut. He watched her closely, seeing the rise and fall of her bosom, knowing that she was beyond control of her emotions.

He said, "I'm Blake Durant."

Therese's mouth gaped. She shook her head slightly, then her sneer came back and with it a renewed buildup of hatred.

"You killed my brother?"

Blake nodded. "He left me no way out."

Therese walked towards him slowly now, her hands at her sides. Blake noted how beautiful she was, even when so disturbed. Her hair fell thick over her shoulders, contrasting with the immaculate whiteness of the silk blouse stretched tight over her high, full breasts. She halted a few feet from him.

"You can stand there and lie to me like that?" she asked. "I'm his sister. My brother could not be shot down by anybody but a filthy coward, somebody who must have tricked him!"

Blake shook his head. "There were plenty of witnesses, ma'am. Come outside and I'll explain the rest of it."

"Explain?" Therese threw at him and then she hurled herself at him. Blake felt the bite of her nails down one cheek before she began to hammer her fists into his face. She was screaming and kicking when he caught her hands and held her away from him.

"Cool down," he told her. "I don't want to hurt you."

"Swine! Filthy, lying scum of a swine!" Therese shouted and renewed her attack so ferociously that Blake was forced to push her against the wall and place a restraining hand in the middle of her back. When she still tried to strike at him, he called to Hap Tonkin:

"You got a room close by where I can put her?"

Tonkin shouted back, "The storeroom. Cleaned it out for some new stock I'm expectin'."

"Show me where it is," Blake said.

Tonkin pulled a ring of keys from his pocket and hurried from behind his counter. Leading the way, he went down a narrow passageway and then he unlocked and opened a door at the end. Standing back, he said, "No windows and the door's double thick."

Blake nodded in satisfaction. He eased Therese into the room and, keeping a firm hold on her, said quietly, "I'll be back when you've got control of yourself. The matter will have to be explained properly to you. There needn't be any hate between us."

Therese spat in his face and tried to sink her teeth into his hands. Tonkin gave her a rough shove and sent her tottering into the room and then he slammed the door closed and locked it. Then Therese cursed and hammered at the door with her fists.

Tonkin said, "That'll hold her for now, Durant. But she ain't stayin' there forever. I don't want that wildcat within a mile of me until she cools down and maybe not even then. You ain't come up against one as wild as her, that I'll swear on."

Blake rubbed his wrists where she had scratched him. He felt a terrible weariness taking hold of him. Looking back up the passageway, he saw the townsmen crowded into the far doorway. His angry eyes sent them back into the saloon to mind their own business. Then he told Tonkin, "I'll stay close until I'm sure she's all right."

"Be a time," Tonkin said. "Therese, she's got a full load of Semole blood in her. If she'd been a man she'd have been worse than either of her brothers. Wild as all get out."

"There's another brother?" Blake asked.

"Kane Semole," Tonkin said.

Blake Durant frowned and Tonkin studied him gravely. "Know him, Durant?"

Blake nodded. "Seems to me I've heard of him."

Tonkin wiped sweat from his brow. "Then there's no need to tell you more, eh? Nico was one thing, and Therese is one thing. But Kane Semole, well …" Tonkin shrugged and went off in a hurry, leaving Blake to make his own way back into the saloon.

# THREE

# ONE MORE HELLION

Ole Manuel inspected the saloon crowd from the bat-wings. His leathery face twisted when he saw Durant keeping his own brooding company in the far corner of the room. Hap Tonkin was busy serving customers, but looked to have no heart in his work. Manuel pushed the doors wide and shuffled in, a terribly old man in ragged clothes. His skin was stretched so tight over his face that it was almost transparent.

Manuel stopped at the bar counter and bought himself a drink. Then, giving the men close to him a severe look, he turned and crossed the room. Drawing up a chair at Durant's table, he sat down without being invited and sipping his drink, he said:

"You don't strike me as a man who'll take advice from many people, Durant, but I'm something kinda special and I'd like you to hear me out."

Blake Durant gave no answer. His weariness had grown in the last hour and he knew it came mostly from the ordeal of waiting. His concern for Therese Semole hadn't helped him much either. In fact, he was beginning to feel a sense of disenchantment with this town.

"I'm special," Manuel said, "because I've been about longer than anybody else in this town, including old Hardy Graham. So, I know more." Manuel sipped at his drink again and wiped his mouth on his grubby sleeve. He eyed the men against the counter with a disdain that interested Durant.

"I've been thirty years in this town, Durant. I've been here since the first wagon train went through and dropped a dozen of us off in the southern valley. I'm the last survivor of that bunch and I guess I've added up to being the least of 'em. Never did make much of myself, mainly because I was never much interested in gettin' no place but where it was comfortable. The job at the jailhouse suits me fine. I eat regular, get somethin' for tobacco and drink and now and again I get a handout of some clothes. Got no complaints."

Blake Durant began to wonder where the old-timer was heading with his talk. But there was nothing better to do, so he let the old man have some rein. Besides, he liked him.

Manuel went on, "Now that's me taken care of. All right, I'll talk about Nico Semole. Nico was his own law in this town, especially when his brother Kane was about. Them two, they didn't give a spit for anybody or anything. They rode roughshod through this town and they told everybody else to go fry. Nico personally killed four men that I know of, and he did it so damn quick and straight out that nobody could hold anything against him. In the beginning Alec Graham went after him, but then Kane bought in, and Alec, finding his hands tied anyway, was forced to back down and bide his time. Only he waited too long. Nico got smart and outwitted him at every turn of the trail, until finally Alec didn't have a leg to stand on and neither did anybody else. Then Kane went on his way but he came back from time to time. Nico was smart—he let it be known that Kane would come back at a whistle from him, so everybody just more or less let Nico have his own way. Until today, when you arrived. Nico was unlucky. You were just too damned good for him."

Blake filled his glass and topped up Ole Manuel's. His gaze went past the old man, traveling along the passageway, at the end of which Therese Semole was still a prisoner. She had ceased to rant and rave and hammer at the door, but Blake was sure she hadn't changed her mind about things.

"Now take Alec Graham," Ole Manuel went on. "Alec was a good lawman once, hard as nails and ready at the jump of a frog to come down on anybody who broke the peace. But then the years caught up with Alec just as they had with old Hardy. Them two, workin' as a team, kept things running smooth in this town, even with Nico and his brother Kane around. So don't think too badly of Alec. He just wasn't good enough to handle Nico and he knew it. If he'd tried, he'd have got himself killed, no doubt on that."

Ole Manuel settled back, pushing at his lips with a grubby forefinger. He seemed to have forgotten that he was talking to Blake Durant as he continued, "Now Therese, she's a real hot one. She's walked in the shadows of her brothers and took every damned comfort she could get. So it makes her as bad as them, and maybe even worse because she ain't even earned any of the things she's demanded from this town as her right. A hellcat, that girl. She steals, deceives, throws

49

herself at respectable men and laughs in their faces when they fall for her bait." Manuel shook his head slowly. "But she's a real woman, the kind hardly any man can ignore. Once she sets her bonnet and body at a man, he's a goner. Watch her real careful, Durant, because she owes everything she is to Nico more'n Kane. She'll get her revenge on you for sure if you give her any kind of a chance."

Blake began to lose interest in the old man's talk, but Ole Manuel was wound up to full gear and there was no stopping him. "But it ain't her you got to really worry about Durant, no sir. Now, you listen to me. You got a fine horse and I can see from your clothes and your manner that you ain't the ordinary run of trail burner on the drift to nowhere. You come from fine folks and maybe you got comforts back home for some reason you're tryin' to forget and stay away from. I don't know and I don't much care. But you helped me when Nico jumped on me and you helped the Graham girl and old Hardy and you stood your ground here against the advice of this town full of damn fools. But the trouble coming your way now, Durant, might be too damned much even for you. Kane Semole, and I'm speaking from the experience of thirty years in this county, is the fastest gun hand who ever threw a shadow over these streets. You're good, but he's like damn greased lightnin'. So, my advice, after tellin' you all that and puttin' things straight, is for you to hang on here, wait for Kane Semole and shoot the stuffin' out of him when he ain't lookin'."

Blake Durant straightened, then he pushed his glass away. "How's that?"

"I said it as plain as I can make it, Durant. You move out and Kane Semole will hunt you down, if it takes him the rest of his life. I don't know what's doggin' your trail this far, but you don't strike me as a man who wants somethin' else on it. Stay and let Kane Semole come for you, and for the good of this town I'll back you up. Old Hardy will, too, because for all his bluster he's dead scared every day of his life that his son, Alec, will break out and try to be the man he once was and get himself killed. The town needs you, Durant."

Blake blew out a loud breath and ran his hands through his corn-colored hair. "That's about the damnedest thing I ever heard in my life, Manuel," he said. "What damned right have you got to—?"

"The right of a man with nothing left in his life but a few friends he admires and respects, no matter if they've slipped downhill some. I seen you punch the hell out of Nico Semole and in that fight you showed yourself as a man who

51

certainly ain't no stranger to trouble. Then the way you didn't bat an eye when Nico came for you with his gun tells me that you got an ability maybe bigger than what you've shown yet. I promise you that you won't have to take Kane Semole on your own. You'll have backing. Then the town will be clear of trouble-makers and some friends of mine will breathe a lot more easily. What have you got to lose?"

"I've got every damn thing to lose," Blake said. "This town means nothing to me."

"You killed a man," Manuel said.

"One who asked for it."

"And you got yourself tied up with his brother and sister. No matter where you go, they'll stalk you, Durant, and finally they'll kill you. So it's best that you make your stand here, where you got some help."

Blake hipped the table away as he got to his feet. He pushed the bottle towards Ole Manuel and said gruffly, "Mister, drink that and keep to hell out of my business."

"Your business is my business, Durant," Manuel said calmly. "Fact is, I got you over a barrel."

Blake frowned down at him. "What do you mean by that, old man?"

Manuel smiled thinly. "I'm just tellin' you how things are. Your horse, that fine big stallion, ain't goin' no place with you, Durant, and from what I seen you ain't the kind who'll leave him behind. Right now he's bein' given the best treatment any horse ever had, only I got him where you won't find him."

Blake Durant stiffened as anger took hold of him. He reached down and grabbed Manuel by the collar. But the old man only grinned and said:

"Hear me out, Durant. This town needs you and I aim to keep you here. I got backing for what I did, believe you me, and there ain't nobody gonna support you against me, no matter what you do. Hurt me all you like, but I reckon you should know by now that I've had my share of hurt in my time and I'm kinda immune to it. You'll have your horse in due time, no fear of that."

Blake shook Manuel roughly. "I'll have it right away, mister," he snapped.

Manuel held his smile. "No, Durant, not even if you kill me. If Kane Semole don't turn up in a few days, you can have him back, sleek and fit and rearin' to go. No other way for it."

Blake pulled Manuel halfway to his feet before he let him drop back to the chair. The old man steadied himself against the table's edge and poured a drink. "Got room for you in the jailhouse, too, Durant—guest of the sheriff and myself and the whole town."

Blake punched one hand into the palm of the other and swore. He noticed that the crowd had gone quiet again. He also noticed that Sheriff Alec Graham was standing just outside the batwings, staring in and frowning, obviously worried about something. Blake Durant returned his attention to Manuel.

"Mister, have my horse saddled and ready for riding at first light in the morning. If you don't, I just might get mad enough to tear this whole town down."

Ole Manuel glanced away and then he grinned at Alec Graham. When Blake made to move from the table, heading for the swing doors, Graham walked quickly down the boardwalk. Durant pushed open the batwings but the sheriff wasn't in sight. Opposite the saloon, Hardy Graham was leaning on his cottage porch rail, the light from the porch showing his huge grin. Blake swore and returned to the saloon. He was damned if he was going to let these towners get away with this. Then, as he burst inside, he heard a woman's screams from down the passageway where Tonkin had locked Therese Semole in the storeroom. Blake stopped short, and saw a worried look reach Tonkin's brow. Ole Manuel had already left the saloon and Blake's bottle had gone with him.

A second scream cut into the room's silence. Blake snapped, "Who the hell's that, mister?"

"A bunch just went that way, Durant. Been here most of the day, sittin' at the end there, drinkin' heavy."

"What bunch?"

"Dobie Martin and his crowd."

"Who the hell's Dobie Martin?" Blake shot at him, his fists closing and impatience riding at him. But then there was still another scream and he waited no longer for Tonkin's information. As he ran into the passageway he heard a loud thud against the wall of the stockroom, the door of which stood open. Turning into the room a few seconds later, he saw first the huge broad back of a cowhand, then the slender form of Therese Semole crouched in fear against the far wall.

The big man was saying, "You been struttin' about too damn long, girl, for my likin'. I had to put up with it before, but no more, not since that scum brother of yours got himself shot up."

The big man reached out and grasped her by the hair. She cried out and slashed her nails at him, digging furrows into his face. He let out a howl of pain and anger, then he tore the blouse from her. Blake Durant took two long strides, pulled the big man around and sent a powerful right hand into his face.

"You swine, Martin!" Therese called out as she used her hands to cover her exposed breasts.

Dobie Martin came off the wall growling a curse. He sent one angry look at Blake Durant and then waded in, thickly muscled arms flailing. Blake stepped to the side and clipped a short left to the jaw which sent Martin's head jolting back. Then Durant went to work on the big man's stomach. Therese jumped out of the way as Martin stumbled across the room, almost crushing her against the wall. She dodged under his right shoulder, shoved Durant away and ran from the room.

Therese's shove did no more than send Blake Durant off balance. But it gave Dobie Martin a chance to recover. He wiped blood away from his gashed mouth and hurled himself forward, getting both hands around Blake Durant's body. Blake felt the fierce power of the huge man doubling him over. Forced back, he went with the thrust of Martin's strength until he could get the support of the side wall. Then he lifted his knee and drove it into Martin's groin. As Martin's fingers spoked open and the pressure left Durant's back, he hammered him to the side, then down, his last blow splitting Martin's cheek to the bone.

Blake Durant stood over him, waiting for him to rise, but the big man's head rolled and then he lay still, his blood seeping into the floorboards.

Taking a deep breath, Durant turned to meet the onrush of men from the saloon. Hap Tonkin was there first, wide-eyed and fearful but doing his best to stem the tide of curious spectators.

"Room!" he barked. "Give Durant room!"

Blake Durant pushed him aside and looked into the back yard. He saw Therese Semole running at full pace down the yard towards the back end of town. Then Sheriff Alec Graham arrived, shouldering his way forward. He took one look at the grim face of Blake Durant and went past him. As he stepped through the doorway, he drew his gun and called:

"You there, Scanlon, Field and Pittwell! Stay put!"

Blake Durant followed the lawman into the yard. Three cowhands were on horses against the far fence. One of them held a spare horse and all three looked nervously back at the lawman.

Then one said, "We had nothing to do with that, Sheriff. We wanted no part of Martin's interest in the girl. Hell, that's the truth—we didn't even try to stop her when she run out of here."

"The three of you ride with Martin," Alec Graham accused them boldly, moving forward with his gun leveled on all three of them. "So what Martin does, you—"

"No," said one of them, the tallest, a red-haired man with a lean body. "We ride with Martin on the range. What the hell else do you expect us to do, workin' for Karl Parry? Karl says clear a section and we do it, with Martin along or not."

"You rode to town with Martin, listened to his damn boasting, of what he coulda done to Nico Semole, didn't you? And didn't you show that you were enjoyin' it? Damn you, Scanlon! Don't lie to me! You knew what he was gonna do, yet you—"

"You know Martin, Sheriff," the lean man went on quickly. "What the hell could we do? If we tried to stop him, he'd have come for us, too. We just said we was cuttin' out and he was on his own. We didn't want no part of Therese or Durant or anybody."

Blake Durant heard murmurs in the crowd gathering in the yard behind him. He studied Scanlon intently for some time before he said, "Sheriff, your jailer has my horse. See that he's in the street at sunup and see that he's fit for travel. As for the rest of it, do what you like with these fools and with that scum inside."

Blake turned away. Alec Graham called his name but Blake ignored him. Then Blake heard him say, "Okay, Scanlon, get your friends and drag Martin outa the saloon and get him the hell outa my town. And by hell see that he don't come back for a week or he'll enjoy the hospitality of my jailhouse. Move now and no damned arguments."

Blake Durant went on his way, cursing. Too much had happened on this one day. He walked into the dark to do some thinking. One thing was settled in his mind. Lincoln had nothing to offer him.

# FOUR

## ANOTHER HOUR OF DARKNESS

Blake Durant heard the board creak at the end of the passageway and got to his feet, gun in hand. He'd been a light sleeper ever since he hit the trail from home, leaving his brother to look after the ranch and tend to his other affairs. But he hadn't slept as lightly for some time as he had this night, remembering the wild hatred of the Semole woman, added to the suspicion that Dobie Martin might not stay out of town as Graham had ordered but would return in the dark to avenge himself.

Blake moved to the door, turned the knob and gave a quick pull. His gun lifted and covered the tall, slender frame of Therese Semole. She gasped and took a step back. Durant saw that she was unarmed, but before he could question her, Alec Graham stepped from the other end of the passageway, his gun covering Therese. The lawman said:

"I've been watching her, Durant, ever since she sent a telegraph message off to her brother Kane in Low Springs. You say the word and I'll put her where she can't bother you or anybody else."

Therese turned a fierce look Graham's way. "You couldn't follow your own feet, lawman, without tripping over them. You think I didn't see you sneaking about and making a fool of yourself? Where did you suddenly get the courage to come out at night, Mr. Big Lawman?"

Graham bit his lip and sucked in his breath. But he came on, straightening tall and trying to show a stubborn front. But Therese ignored him and confronted Blake Durant.

"I came to talk to you," she said.

"About what?" Blake asked.

"Nico's death and also about my other brother. It's you who needs things explained to you, Mr. Durant, not me. I know now what happened. I heard it all from people I can trust."

Alec Graham ran the end of his gun over his jaw and muttered, "I wouldn't trust her if she was tied hand and foot, Durant. I'm tellin' you, the Semole breed is—"

"Be quiet!" Therese snarled. "I'm talking to Mr. Durant, the only man in this town with the courage to come to a woman's aid when she was being molested by one of your big brave citizens. You call yourself a sheriff!" She spat. "You make me want to vomit!"

Alec Graham swallowed hard and looked at Durant.

"It's all right," Blake said.

"To hell it is, Durant. I'm warnin' you—"

"I don't need your warnings," Blake cut in. "So far, Graham, I've managed to take care of my own affairs in your town. I think I still can." He stepped aside and invited Therese into the room. She hesitated; then, seeing Graham make no effort to move off, she lifted her head arrogantly, threw him a disdainful look and moved past Durant.

Alec Graham came another step forward, clearly not yet ready to drop the matter, but Durant said, "Just see that my horse is where I said it should be, Graham, and also see that your jailer and your father don't get any loco notions to get in my hair again. As I see it, you've got a town botched to the limit and you can have it."

Blake slammed the door in Graham's face and turned to look at Therese Semole. She had changed into a light skirt and had replaced her torn blouse. She'd evidently spent a bit of time prettying herself up. She wore a shade too much cheek rouge and her lips glistened wetly. But the overuse of makeup did nothing to lessen her solemn beauty as her dark eyes took in Durant.

"Do you have a drink here, Mr. Durant?"

"No."

Therese smiled tightly and said, "I don't suppose I really need one anyway. It's just that lately I've depended on drink to tolerate myself and those around me. I've been such a fool. All of us have been such fools."

"All?" Blake said.

Her gaze was firmly fixed on him. He saw that her fiery spirit remained, ready to be touched off. Given the slightest provocation, she'd come tearing at him again. While she remained quiet he was prepared to go along with her.

"Yes, we've been fools," she said. "Myself, my brother Nico, and my brother Kane. After you saved me from that animal, Martin, I ran and ran. Then I broke down in my room and for the first time in my life I wished to be dead. Nico's death upset me terribly and I hated you and meant to kill you. But then I was advised by some friends

who saw you in action to take care. None of them
wanted to go after you. So I sent for Kane."

Blake nodded, sat on the bunk and continued his study of her. He put her down at being
no more than twenty years of age, perhaps even
younger. He'd often been deceived by the age of
dark-skinned women.

"Kane will come," she said. "And he will kill
you. So you must leave town, right away."

"You're telling me to run?" Blake asked in surprise. Therese walked towards him and stopped
only a pace away, her dark eyes mirrors of sincerity. Her perfume flowed across to Durant and
made him think of pines along a creek, with lush
grass beyond the timber blowing in a cool breeze.

"Yes, Mr. Durant, as I said, I wanted to kill you.
But that was before I sat down with friends and
was given a full explanation of what happened
between you and Nico. I've always been at Nico to
leave the Graham girl alone. She is not for him.
She is too prim and proper and shallow for a man
of Nico's spirit. She did not want him and never
would have wanted him. But Nico had his heart set
on taming her, and today, when he really meant
to have her, come what may, he was wrong."

Blake settled back on the pillow, looking
relaxed but ready to ward off an attack if she
was merely trying to catch him off-guard. But

Therese rested her hip against his bedside table and pushed back her hair. There was warmth in her eyes and her lips looked soft, so very soft.

"Nico should not have forced himself on her," she said. "And he should not have gone after you because you beat him up. But he was always so proud, and so sure of himself. I told him time after time that one day he would meet his match. I've lain awake at nights, wondering where he was, what he was up to and whether he would come home or be found in the morning lying on the ground with a bullet in his back."

Her eyes narrowed and a nerve jumped at her temple as her lips thinned. Blake watched her carefully. Then her show of anger passed.

"You shot him only because he forced you to," she said. "I was told that by people I trust. And then, when you helped me against that pig, Martin, I understood better the kind of man you are, somebody Nico gave no choice to, somebody who would have been undeservedly dead if Nico had had his way."

Her shoulders slumped and she turned and looked out the window into the rooming house yard. She was silent for a long time before she let out a deep sigh and turned to look at him again.

"I hate this town, Mr. Durant. I've always hated it, yet I've stayed on. The men here think less of me than they would a cheap dance hall girl who sleeps with all men who can pay for her body." Her eyes sparked with resentment. "But they have not been able to have their way with me. Oh, they've made plenty of proposals and I've accepted their drinks and their food and their flattery, but not one of them has been able to take me, to use my body for his filthy hands to … to …"

Therese gave a shallow laugh and sent her long hair flying with a toss of her head. In the room's dim light her skin shone like dark satin.

"They were all afraid. They wanted me but were so terribly frightened of my brothers that they held back. Yes, they were stirred up so much they couldn't keep their eyes off me or free their minds of foul thoughts—but they did not touch me. So instead they hated me and told lies about me."

Therese moved about the room now, taking in the gunbelt looped over the top of the bed, Durant's boots placed side by side under the bed, his shaving gear on the table top. She picked up the razor and made a pretence of shaving herself. She gave another laugh.

Then seriously, "I hate this town so much and everybody in it that I feel sick to my stomach. And now Nico is dead and Kane is coming." Therese moved close to him and placed a hand lightly on his shoulder. "I do not blame you for killing Nico. I know now that it had to come sooner or later. I think I always knew, inside, that Nico would be killed while still young. I think, too, that he knew it. That was why he never backed down from any man. He was always trying to live in Kane's image, but he did not have Kane's ability."

She licked her lips and studied Blake gravely. Her lips trembled and suddenly the hand on his shoulder tightened.

"Mr. Durant, please leave this town. Kane will come very soon and he will kill you. I am tired of all the fighting and hating and killing. This town means nothing to you and nothing to me. Let us go, together, while we can. Later, we can decide what's best for both of us to do. I will not be in your way, I promise you."

Blake straightened. "Even if I wanted to, Miss Semole," he told her, "I couldn't."

"Why couldn't you? Surely you do not have the pride of my brother Nico. Please, do not be like those who wait for death."

"I do what I like when I like, ma'am," Blake said. "I can't leave now. My horse is lame."

Therese studied him more intently. "From what Nico did to it?"

Blake nodded.

"How long will it be before you can leave?"

"I don't know, Miss Semole."

She frowned and moved back a pace. "They said the buckboard only struck your horse lightly."

"I just don't know," Blake said and came to his feet. Therese moved closer, her hands at her waist. Her look softened and an expression of deep sincerity came into her face. For a moment color rose in her cheeks, then she said: "I need you, can you understand that? You killed my brother but I still want you. I need a man like you. I've known so many bad, evil men—thieves and killers who rode with my brothers. I've had to care for them, tend their wounds, listen to their foul talk." Tears came into her eyes and she moved against him, pressing her firm breasts against his chest. She looked into his eyes and a tear rolled down her cheek. "I loved Nico. He was not as bad as they said he was. He was wild and reckless and he cared nothing much for other people. But he did his fighting in the open. He had rules he abided by. Kane is different. He is mean and vicious and nobody knows him. I've never been close to him and I don't care where he goes or what happens to him. But I do care what happens to you ... and to me." Her hands

moved over Blake's shoulders, caressingly, sending a tingle through him. He wanted to push her
away, then stayed his hands. He couldn't bring
himself to hurt her any more.

He said, "When will your brother come?"

"Tomorrow, Mr. Durant, I'm sure of it. Please
let's go before then. He'll never find us, I'll see
to that."

She was leaning hard against him now, her
hands firm on his broad shoulders. Her lips
parted and a deep sigh came from her. Blake
Durant remembered another beautiful woman
standing like this, so close that he could feel
every curve of her body, a woman who wanted to
give all of herself to be his unconditionally.

He eased Therese back as gently as he could,
"Miss Semole, I can't help you."

A change worked into Therese's face, harden-
ing it. "Can't or won't, Mr. Durant?"

"Can't."

"Then you'll leave me at the mercy of the
scum in this town. You think what Martin wanted
to do, a lot of others won't try also, now that
Nico can no longer help me and protect me?
Don't you know yet what the men in this town
are like—cowards, lustful, brutal men who sneak
and gape and have thoughts that would turn a
decent woman sick?"

Blake shook his head. "I'm afraid it's none of my business, Miss Semole. Take my advice and go see Sheriff Graham. I'm sure he'll protect you, provided you behave yourself."

Therese's face colored quickly. She drew back a hand and stood poised, as if to strike him, the hand raised and her eyes flashing in anger. Blake stared into her eyes and suddenly she sighed and her hand fell to her side. She turned and walked hurriedly to the door and pulled it open. She stepped out but stopped in the passageway.

"Kane will kill you if you stay," she said. "My cottage is the last house at the end of this street. It will take me only a few minutes to pack if you change your mind. I need you, Mr. Durant. I'll go any place with you, do anything you want me to. I can work and I can be a woman better than any you have ever known."

Despite himself Blake found his gaze moving up and down her body. Therese, conscious of his interest in her, rushed back and threw herself into his arms. She kissed him hard, then she broke free and ran out.

Blake stood there for a long time, looking at the empty doorway. He lifted a hand and touched his lips, his mind returning him to another time and another place, another woman. Finally he pushed the thoughts away and kicked the door closed. When he stretched out on the bunk he found he was no longer tired.

Hardy Graham opened the door of Durant's room just on sunup the next morning. He carried his old rifle and was wearing a battered campaign hat with a feather in the band. He was clean-shaven and bright-eyed.

"Bugle call, Durant," he shouted out and pushed past his son, Sheriff Alec Graham, who waited hesitantly in the passageway outside the room.

Blake Durant lifted his gun above the blanket and the old man frowned at first, taking a backward step, then his face broke into a wide grin. He nudged his son in the ribs with the rifle and said excitedly:

"There, boy, I told you, didn't I? Got the stamp of a good man about him, always on the alert. By hell, a few more like you with Custer and myself, Durant, and we'd have whipped the Injuns to a frazzle and taken over this frontier years earlier than we did."

The old man pounded into the room and pulled Durant's blankets away. "Up, man, up. Work to be done."

"What the hell do you want?" Blake said, trying to be annoyed, but unable to feel any real animosity towards this old fool.

"I want a talk, young man, with you. By hell, last night I had my thoughts all mixed up. But a good sleep, a good think about you and the trouble coming our way, then I decided too much time was being lost gettin' to know you. My granddaughter is puttin' on the best breakfast you ever saw. While we eat it and get to know each other, we can work out a plan of defense."

Blake pushed himself to his feet. "Defense against who?"

Hardy Graham pulled at his whiskers and eyed Blake frowningly. "Why, Kane Semole, of course, Durant. Ain't you heard? He's comin'. Should be here today or tomorrow at the latest. He's down at Low Springs and provided he's got his business affairs in order, he'll be comin' straight here. Ain't more'n seventy miles as the buzzards fly, Durant." Blake reached for his shirt and put it on. After lacing up his boots and buckling on his gunbelt, he washed up in the corner basin. Then he checked his gun and watched as Alec Graham finally entered the room.

"What we really came for, Durant, is to convince you, for your own good and the good of the town, to light out, Then, when Kane Semole comes, we can send him after you, but on a false trail."

Blake eyed him sharply. "You'd tell the big man a lie, Graham?"

Alec Graham licked his lips nervously and coughed into his hand. He looked about as miserable as Blake had ever seen him.

"Hell, Durant, why not? You help us and we'll help you."

"Quiet, boy," said Hardy Graham sternly. "Leave this to me. Mr. Durant isn't going any place. Why should he run from scum like Kane Semole today and then get shot in the back someplace else? Durant," old Hardy went on, turning his back on the sheriff, "we don't want you to leave. We want you to stay and to hell with this gun punk, Kane Semole. I give you my word," he added, straightening to his full height and trying to assume a young man's military bearing, "that I'll back you to the limit. Been too much molly-coddlin' here and lettin' hellions run this town. It's high time we set about being men with guts instead of sniveling damned little puny—"

"Now wait a minute, Pa," put in Alec Graham. "You said—"

"What I said before doesn't count, son. I've done a lot of clear thinking since then. We owe Durant a debt and I intend to see that it gets paid.

Let Kane Semole come. I'll be there, as I was with Custer, as I was with General Coe and Brigadier Moses and the settlers along the Platte in the early days, waitin' for them redskins to come hollerin' down, drunk on white man's whisky and out to scalp us and take off our women and kids. By hell!" Hardy Graham thumped his fist into the palm of his left hand. "I've stood against a hangin' mob when they threatened a friend of mine, and I put 'em back on their heels. I tossed Ben Younger, pa of those wild Younger boys, on the flat of his back for lookin' at me the wrong way." He began to pace the room, his face becoming more flushed as he raved on. "I've tamed more men in my time and more towns than the present generation could count in an hour's totin' up. Do you think for one minute that a glassy-eyed, puny little punk like Kane Semole can come here into my town and take it by the horns and throw it how he likes? No, by hell, no!"

"Kane Semole is no puny brat," Alec Graham corrected his perspiring father. "Semole is over six feet tall and as wide as a doorway. He's the fastest, most vicious, meanest damned—"

"Punk and runt and scum!" roared the old man.

Blake Durant moved to the door and held it open. "If you're going to rant and rave, how about using the street?" Graham eyed him sternly for a short time before he stomped through the doorway. Alec followed but Blake grasped his arm and whirled him around.

"Where'd you put my horse, Graham?"

The lawman's face went red. He shook his head. "I haven't touched it, mister."

Blake sucked in his breath angrily. "Now listen here, Graham. I've had enough of this town. Either you give up my horse or I'll get the idea that the Semole boys haven't done enough hell-raisin' here to suit anybody. Where is my horse, damn you?"

"My jailer, Ole Manuel, took it off, Durant. I admit I knew he was gonna do it, to delay you a while. But this morning, when I'd decided you'd be better off if you hit the trail, I went looking for Manuel. I don't know where he is or where he's put your horse. That's the honest truth of it, Durant."

Blake bit off an oath and turned to the old man. "Do you know, Graham?"

"If I did I wouldn't tell you, Durant. I want you to stay. I want this town to see what happens when a man stands his ground. I want you to give 'em an example they can look up to and maybe live by. Like I said, I'll be right there alongside you, expectin' others to follow suit. When this is over, maybe my boy will have the ready support of men no longer afraid of being killed."

Blake scrubbed a hand across his face and sighed as Hardy Graham led his son to the top of the stairs. The old man turned and called back:

"No sense in wastin' good grub, Durant. My granddaughter wants to thank you for helpin' her yesterday evenin'. I don't think a man like you will find spendin' some time in her company all that hard to stomach."

With a grin the old man went off at a spritely pace. But Alec Graham shrugged clear of him and stayed behind. Seeing Durant's face go into a heavy frown, he said, "We'll eat and then go and look for your horse. Manuel won't buck me for long. We'll get your horse and then you can be on your way."

"It better be like that," Blake told him, then he went down the stairs.

Outside, Blake saw the Graham girl standing on the porch of the Graham house, her hair blowing back under the sweep of a gentle breeze. When she saw the three men she sent a smile across the street and then she hurried inside.

# FIVE

# A GUNHAND WAITS

The early morning sunlight bleached out the porch of the cottage, its brightness making the doorway seem even darker. Blake Durant, blinded momentarily, couldn't make out any details of the house's interior until he had stood for a while just inside the doorway, rubbing a spot of grime off his range hat. Then he sighted the slender young woman at the stove, her long, glossy hair neatly brushed back and tied with a yellow ribbon. She moved gracefully, efficient and feminine, stirring a memory of another woman at a stove making his dinner. On that far-off day Louise's family had gone to town, leaving them alone. That was the day he proposed to Louise Yerby. The next day she was dead.

Joy Graham turned and old Hardy Graham walked to her, stripped the apron off her waist and tossed it aside. Smiling in his superior way, he led her back across the room.

"Joy, this is Blake Durant. You ain't exactly met properly but I reckon you should get to know each other. Durant's come for some grub and a talk about the trouble loomin' up for us and the rest of the town."

Blake Durant had already read more into the place than Joy Graham would have believed. Everything was in its place. The drapes were hung just right and there was no dust on the furniture or the shelves. Not even the smell of the cooking disturbed the fresh fragrance of the house. It was a homely place, kept perfectly by someone who cared.

"I'm pleased to know you, Mr. Durant," Joy said with a shy smile. "And I'm also pleased to have the opportunity to thank you for saving me from that—" Her voice trailed off.

"From that low-bellied scum, Nico Semole!" Hardy Graham finished for her.

Alec Graham, after removing his hat, had carefully brushed his boots in the doorway and had taken a seat on the divan. Now he was perched on its edge as if afraid he might soil something.

"He deserved to die!" Hardy Graham roared. "I'd have killed him myself if you hadn't, Durant!"

Joy's face went red at her grandfather's words.

Durant saved her further embarrassment by saying quietly, "The whole thing was unfortunate. It would have been better for all concerned if it had not happened."

"I know," Joy said, her eyes meeting Blake's gaze. "Nico Semole was a distasteful person, but I certainly didn't wish him dead. If only he could have controlled himself …"

Durant said, "It's over with, ma'am. I think it's best that we all try to forget it."

"Yes." Joy drew in a sigh and took a step towards the stove. "Is your horse all right?" she asked.

Durant glanced at Alec Graham who was still on the divan, looking uncomfortable.

"I expect that my horse is in good shape," Blake said. Old Hardy, his eyes darting about as if he sensed trouble close by, walked heavily across the room and sniffed at the bacon and eggs frying in the skillet.

"Could eat a horse, girl," he said. "The sooner you put some solid linin' into our stomachs, the sooner we can get down to makin' our plans.

79

Speed it up now, Joy, so we can talk better later on."

Hardy Graham came between Joy and Durant, giving Durant the opportunity to take better stock of him. The old man's eyes were gleaming with self-satisfaction, a fact that annoyed Blake more than a little. Then Joy brought three heaped plates to the table. Alec Graham rose from the divan and sat beside old Hardy at the table. Durant stood behind a chair and looked at Joy.

"Miss Graham …"

She smiled and said, "I've already eaten, Mr. Durant. Please sit down."

Blake sat and started on his meal. The breakfast bacon was crisp, the eggs fresh and the hot biscuits light and deep-crusted. When he finished, Blake accepted a second cup of coffee and leaned back, making a cigarette and smiling at Joy. Hardy Graham watched them with keen interest for a time before he gave Alec a wink and got to his feet.

"Well, Durant, you might not have business to attend to, but we have. While Alec's trackin' down Manuel and seeing to it that your horse is all right, I've got some people to talk to and arrange some business affairs with. Later, when the saloon's open for business, we'll meet up with you there. That suit you all right?"

"I'll see you," Blake said as Hardy stepped across to Joy to give her a light kiss on the forehead.

"Be back as soon as I can, girl. Don't you fret now, not about anything."

Blake saw concern in Joy's small-featured face and he decided that if he was being left alone with the girl for some ulterior motive, she had no part in it. Her flushed cheeks and obvious nervousness told him this.

"About an hour, Durant," Hardy said from the doorway as he pushed his son ahead of him. "Take your time—enjoy your smoke and the coffee."

Then he was gone. Joy stood wiping her hands on her apron and looking at the closed door.

Blake stood for a moment, then sat down and sipped at his coffee, letting his unlit cigarette hang limp in the fingers of his left hand. He studied her as she struggled to compose herself, then helped her out by saying, "The old boy takes long strides in any direction that suits him."

Joy slowly picked up his meaning and smiled shyly. "He's always been like that. Once he gets his mind made up about something, nothing can stop him."

"Seems to have his son hogtied a bit too much," Blake told her, before sitting back and lighting his cigarette.

"Yes." Joy returned to the kitchen and began to wash the breakfast dishes.

Durant brought his empty mug to her and reached for the dish towel. "I'll do it," she said. "You go and sit down."

"I'm no stranger to home chores, ma'am," Durant said easily. "And, like your grandfather said, without my horse I'm not going any place just yet."

"They've taken your horse?" Joy asked.

"I don't know about the 'they' part, ma'am," Blake said. "From what I've been told, the jailer, Ole Manuel, took my horse so I wouldn't leave town. But I'm not past putting your grandfather or your father into the business either."

The smile in his voice kept Joy from being upset by the inference in his words. "Why would they do that?" she asked, apparently unable to relax with Blake standing so close to her.

Blake shrugged. "I can see only one answer to that, ma'am, the one I just gave you—to keep me in town. But it seems your father has changed his mind. Now he thinks I should shift on. Your grandfather, though, has some plan to keep me in town so I'll be here when Kane arrives."

"Kane Semole?" The name came sharply from her throat. Her forehead grew sudden lines and her hands stopped moving in the washing-up water.

"That's right," Blake said. "Nico's brother, Kane. His sister sent for him when I killed Nico. Seems they were a close-knit family."

Joy licked at her lips nervously. Then, after a moment of deep thought, she said, "Grandfather is impossible sometimes. He lives so much in the past. If I were you, Mr. Durant, I'd take more notice of my father than of my grandfather: Grandpa has a one-track mind when he gets started on something. If you demand that they return your horse, I'm positive that my father will see you get it right away. He's not the kind of man who—"

"He's the kind of man who should throw in his badge," Blake said grimly. He saw anger rise in her face, but then she bit at her lip and nodded.

"Yes, I—I'm afraid you're right about that. He doesn't even want the job. Pa has done too much fighting in his day. He wants peace now. He wants to get a normal job, to be treated like other people, to be part of the town—not a man forced to stand on his own …"

"Then why doesn't he quit?" Blake asked as he placed a stack of plates on the shelf behind the stove. When he turned to face her she studied him intently as if trying to make up her mind about him.

"Quit?" Joy asked, and frowned. "The way you said that … well, it sounds like you think it's something a coward would do."

"No," Blake said. "Cowardice has nothing to do with it. I just feel that when a man can no longer do his job, he should get out."

"Pa can do his job," Joy said angrily. "You've no right to condemn him like that when—"

"It's no condemnation," Blake said easily. "Just a straight look at the facts. By his own admission your father couldn't handle the Semole brothers. When a lawman can't stay on top of trouble-makers, when he doesn't want to lock horns with them and accept the risks involved in controlling them, then he shouldn't be in office. He should be doing something easier, something less dangerous."

An angry flush came to Joy's cheeks. "He is no coward!" she snapped.

Blake shrugged. "Didn't say he was. But he's out of his depth, Miss Graham. The way I see it, a woman like you, caught up in his affairs as you are, should be the first to tell him that and try and coax him into leaving his position honorably."

Joy's face went white. She struggled to find the right words to counter what she obviously thought was an unfair attack on her father, but she couldn't stand up to this expressionless man who said what he thought. This sense of power and his self confidence stopped her, yet with almost any other man she could more than hold her own. But she had to protect her father's reputation, his good name, and finally she found her voice.

"My father has done a great deal for this town. When he was younger—"

But he cut her off. "He's through and it's time he admitted it to himself. Why doesn't he?"

"He knows, Mr. Durant, he knows. But what can he do, when grandpa is so stubbornly opposed to pa's retiring. Grandpa has such deep pride that he won't even listen to my father. And pa can't let himself disgrace grandpa."

"Disgrace?" Blake said. "What does that have to do with anything? Your father's done his job, but he's lost his punch. It's a job that demands a young man's drive and initiative. If your father stays in it he can get killed. Is that the pride you and your father want to feel?"

"Not me and not my father. But my grandfather—he'd disown pa if he turned in his badge."

Blake put down the last of the dishes, wiped his hands and handed Joy the towel. He said, "Somebody should tell your grandfather to mind his own business, ma'am." He walked across the room and picked up his hat. Joy was still regarding him frowningly when he turned back to her. "Can't you do that, Miss Graham? Can't you tell your menfolk to wake up to themselves before it's too late?"

Joy pinched her lips and closed her eyes momentarily. "You think I haven't tried, Mr. Durant? I've set out to do that dozens of times, but neither of them will hear me out." Hope entered her eyes. "Perhaps they might listen to you."

Blake shook his head. "Nothing I've said in this town got much of a hearing, ma'am. No, I think it's your business and you'll have to work it out. The meal was fine. I'm obliged."

He walked to the door and held it open, letting the warm breeze come in from the porch. The town still held an attraction for him, with the prairie and hill country beyond casting spells of its own. He scrubbed a hand onto the back of his neck and began to walk. He was near the gate when he heard her come onto the porch. He turned as she spoke.

"My father will listen to you, Mr. Durant. I know he considers you to be an honest and brave man. He wouldn't have brought you home otherwise. And as for my grandfather, for all his wild talk and boasting, he's not nearly the man he still thinks himself to be. He'll also listen to you, I'm sure."

Blake eyed her thoughtfully for some time before he shrugged. "I might say something." He went into the street. When he looked back from the boardwalk he saw her standing on the porch, the beginning of a smile working at her lips. He realized then that whatever use her menfolk might have planned to make of her, the young woman had turned the meeting to her own advantage. Now he was committed to solve another problem. He swore under his breath, then he turned across the street and entered the livery stable lane way. Walking along with the warm wind in his face, he was suddenly aware that the town was quiet; the activity of yesterday was missing. Only a few people were moving about. The feel of the tension in the air reminded him that a man was coming to kill him. Blake hooked his gunbelt higher on his waist and strode on. When he reached the livery stable and saw Sundown being exercised in the yard, he stopped dead in his tracks.

Sundown was circling the yard on a halter held by Ole Manuel. Manuel's voice was a soothing drawl in the morning's quiet and the horse seemed content. Which surprised Blake. Few men were able to get that close to Sundown, and he doubted if it was because the stallion was still favoring his left foreleg.

Blake stood at the rails and watched. Sundown trotted past him, then turned his head sharply, whirled and pulled Manuel across to the rails. As Blake lifted a hand and stroked the big black's nose, Ole Manuel came behind the horse, shifted him gently aside and said:

"Easy now, boy, you still got to watch that leg some."

Blake eyed the little dark-skinned man intently, then Manuel went on:

"I've given him a good rub-down with liniment. I spent half the night doing that. The horse gave me no trouble."

"He's got good sense," Blake said,

"He's just about the smartest horse I've handled, Durant, and I've taken care of hundreds in my time. He seems to know exactly what a man says to him."

"Once he wrote a book," Blake said with a grin. "It told what horses had to do to get out of a corral. It was never published because I figured horse owners would object."

"Pity," Manuel said. "Would have sold a lot of copies."

Manuel turned the horse about and pushed at his hindquarters, then the big black circled the yard again for Blake's inspection. Manuel stood, turning with the pull of the short halter, and speaking quietly. "You can still see the swelling. Two more rubs and a little heat and he should be right by morning."

Blake waited until Manuel had stopped Sundown again before he asked, "Why hide him on me, mister?"

Manuel's black eyes settled on him. "Because I respect and admire Alec Graham a great deal. He's a good man."

"Past his prime," Blake said.

Manuel nodded his acceptance of this. "Sure, well past. Past, that is, if you're talkin' about shoot-outs with the likes of Nico and Kane Semole. But he's still a good man, trustworthy and keen at his job, a lawman who can keep control under normal circumstances. It was because of Alec mostly that I wanted to have you about when that killer Kane Semole arrives. You can take him, Durant, and do a lot of people a favor."

"It's not rightly my business," Blake said.

"You killed his brother."

"If he has any sense he should know that was bound to happen."

Manuel smiled tolerantly. "Kane Semole hasn't got any sense, at least not the way you mean it. He's got animal cunning and brutality in him. He packs a punch with hand or gun that will take a real good man to beat. I think you're that man."

Blake swore under his breath and studied Sundown again. What he had just seen convinced him that the horse needed another day's rest. And he didn't intend going anywhere without the big black.

He said quietly, "You'll stay with the horse, Manuel?"

"Day and night, Durant."

"And have him ready when I come for him?"

"No matter when. I was wrong leading him off the last time. I don't expect there'll be a need to do it again."

Blake accepted this and stroked Sundown again. He stayed with the horse for several minutes and then went on his way. As he turned into the main street, he sighted Dobie Martin entering a side street at the other end of the town. Blake stopped as Martin glanced in his direction.

But Dobie Martin did no more than grin crookedly before continuing on.

Blake Durant felt a chill run the length of his spine. He had met many men of Martin's stripe. He felt no fear of them but he knew Martin's breed would do anything to revenge humiliation. His kind thrived on what bullying could bring them. When someone came along to put such a bully in his place, he looked for ways to get even and regain his lost prestige. Blake stepped off the boardwalk, and then Alec Graham came across the street, looking in Martin's direction.

"He lost his job," Graham said.

"How come?"

"Karl Parry, the man he worked for, is one of the old breed. He has a mighty respect for womenfolk. When some of his boys explained the kind of trouble Martin had got mixed up in, old Karl just paid him up and kicked him off his place."

"Good man," Durant said. "Martin's a bad apple. If he worries me again, Sheriff, I won't answer for what happens."

"He knows that, Durant. Martin has never been more than a bully. I doubt if he'll tackle you again. If he does, I guess it's his mistake."

"You're going to let him stay in town?"

"Why not? He took his beating and he has money. I've got no reason yet to shift him on.

But if he makes trouble, I'll move him out. You have my word on that."

Blake wiped a line of sweat from his face. It was getting too warm to be standing in the sun. He shifted back to the shade of the boardwalk and Graham followed him.

"What about Kane Semole?" the lawman finally asked, tugging his gunbelt into place.

"What about him, Sheriff?"

"Hell come, no doubt of that."

Blake shrugged. "My horse isn't ready for riding yet." And with that he went on. When he turned into the Tonkin saloon, Alec Graham crossed the street to his house and found his father sitting on the porch cleaning his ancient gun.

The old man's shrewd eyes took in his son's look and said, "He's stayin' on then?"

"Horse ain't right."

"See Manuel and make sure it ain't right for another two days. Kane Semole might just take his time coming, might want to check things out. If he talks to his sister first, she'll tell him how it was, fair and square. Knowing Durant's no slouch with a gun will put him on his guard. So it might take longer than I expected before he makes his move."

Alec Graham, tight-lipped, suddenly said, "I'm not tellin' Ole Manuel to do anything, Pa.

Durant's horse is still sore but as soon as it's fit to travel, Durant will be informed about it. And I don't want you buttin' in and doin' anythin' loco, Pa. I won't have any more of your interferin'."

Hardy Graham stiffened and sat forward with a jerk.

"Did I hear you right, boy? Are you tellin' me that—?"

"I'm tellin' you plain and straight, Pa. I'm not bein' part of settin' Durant up to be shot down. If he stays of his own accord, well and good, but by hell I'll be no party to keeping him in town against his will. Neither will you."

Hardy Graham jumped to his feet and pounded the rifle stock on the floorboards. His face was livid with rage and he spluttered for a moment before he blurted out, "Boy, have you lost control of your senses, talkin' to me like that?"

"I'm tellin' you as plain as I can, Pa, to mind your own damn business. And when Kane Semole comes, stay in the house. I don't want you buyin' in, settin' off any fuses. This ain't the Platte and it ain't Custer's army and there ain't a Redskin within a hundred miles of us. So just sit and chew on your cud and leave the town's business to me."

Alec Graham, his face as flushed as his father's, turned and strode briskly down the street, leaving the old man cursing a treat at his back. But Joy came onto the porch a few minutes later and placed a firm hand on the old man's bowed shoulders.

"Don't, Grandpa," she said gently.

"You hush yourself, girl!" the old man retorted. "Impudent young pup! I spent a lifetime rearin' him and now I see him stand and abuse me, call me an old, interferin' fool. By hell—!"

"You reared him to be a lawman and he's being that, Grandpa. Pa knows what he has to do. If he needs you, he'll come for you, I'm sure."

"If?"

Joy turned him around. "He's so much like you, Grandpa. He has his pride, too. Do you want to take that away from him?"

Hardy Graham's rage abated and he eased back from her. "Pride?" he said. "What are you talkin' about, girl?"

"He's the sheriff of this town, Grandpa. He has to have full authority and he can't have that when you're interfering. Now come inside. I've got your coffee on."

Joy returned to the house and left the door open. She heard him still grumbling after that, but when he finally came in his face was grey and heavy with thought. He looked morosely at her and then he slumped down in his chair and put his gnarled old hands around the coffee mug. Not looking at her, he sat there, hunched over, an old man who had finally taken a good look at himself and realized he had only memories left.

# SIX

# A TOWN WAITS

Dobie Martin didn't make an appearance in the saloon until sundown. He used the back door and took a long look at the customers standing along the counter before he brought his bruised and battered body to the end of the bar. He tossed his money on the counter and stared at Hap Tonkin without saying a word. Hap Tonkin served him silently took his money and left Martin to his brooding.

At about this time Blake Durant inspected his horse and found that Sundown had almost completely recovered under Manuel's skilled attention. By morning Sundown would be his own frisky self and ready for any trail Blake Durant set him along. Blake walked to the saloon and was

96

halfway to the bar when he sighted Martin. Their eyes met and the big man's bruised face scowled. Blake bellied up to the bar beside Martin and bought a drink. Looking into his glass, he said, "Want to see me, mister?"

Martin's lips curled back in a sneer. "I don't ever want to see you any place, Durant. I got my rights to be here same as anybody else."

"Do you bear me a grudge, mister?"

Martin stepped away from the bar counter. His hips were gunless. He said, "Sure, I bear you a grudge, Durant. What do you expect?"

"You intend to do anything about it?"

"Nope." Martin chuckled, hooked himself over the counter and shifted his glass in a pool of rye. "Nope, I ain't gonna do a damned thing, Durant. One thing I learned from kicking my heels in towns like this was to steer clear of any-body too damned good for me. Mr. Big Man, I figure you're just too fast with a gun for me, and you hit too damned hard. So, I'm just gonna leave you be."

"That's the most sensible thing you've ever decided in your life, Martin," Blake told him, feeling an edge of uneasiness shifting through him. The day's waiting had got on his nerves and the way the townspeople kept their distance weighed heavily on him.

"Yeah, I'm bein' real sensible, Durant. I'm just gonna wait about and watch it when it happens." Dobie Martin turned, pushing an elbow onto the counter and lifting his glass in a salute to Durant. "Gonna watch it from the side, Durant, and see your guts blown out. You ever see Kane Semole in action?"

Blake straightened. "I don't give a spit about Kane Semole."

"Well, you should, drifter. Nico, he was good, fast as a blur. You were just a tick in front of him, as I saw it. But Kane, by hell, he'd pick Nico up by the seat of his pants and spank him. He'll take you, Durant, and I'm gonna stand and watch it."

Blake grabbed a handful of Martin's shirt and pulled him in close. "Don't push your luck," he said. "I don't like the look of you or the stink of you or the sound of you. Maybe you should find another town."

Blake pushed and let go of the dirty shirt. Martin staggered back and said:

"You go to hell, Durant. You don't own this town. I already saw the sheriff and he says I can stay. So you leave me be."

"Then shut down and keep out of my sight. I don't intend to let you come within shooting distance of me while I'm in this town. Do you hear me? Keep beyond shooting distance. Any closer

98

and I just might get the idea you're gunning for me and behave accordingly."

Martin slapped his hips. "I got no gun, Durant. I ain't wearin' one now and I won't be wearin' one while you're about. If you draw on me, you'll draw on a defenseless man and it'll be called murder."

Blake eyed him with disgust and pushed him aside. "You heard what I said," he told him and moved back along the bar.

Every eye in the room turned to Martin and stayed fixed on the big drifter as he moved across the room. After studying four card players grimly, he pulled up a chair, dropped some money in front of him and growled, "Deal me in."

The card players exchanged quick looks before the dealer shrugged and started to shuffle the cards. At the bar, Blake Durant was staring into his third drink when a gun exploded in the main street.

Hap Tonkin looked at Durant. "Came from near direct across from here."

Several men hurried to the batwings and crowded together there.

"Well, what the hell is it?" Hap Tonkin called. "You see anythin'?"

Two of the men shook their heads but the third, peering through squinted eyes over the batwings, said tightly, "I see only old Hardy Graham out there. He's—"

There was a second gunshot and the man at the batwings stepped back quickly, his face going pale. He turned shocked eyes on Blake Durant and said, "Kane Semole."

Blake joined the rush of men and pushed his way to the boardwalk. Somehow he sensed that this was his business, that Kane Semole, by firing off the shots, was in effect, throwing down the gauntlet for him to pick up.

Then somebody called, "Over there against the fence. Old Hardy—he's been shot!"

Blake saw the old man drag himself to his feet, stagger into his yard fence and fall again. Up the street, Joy Graham and her father came running. Blake went into a sprint, reaching the old man before they did. He lifted the grey head from the weeds against the fence and studied the lined, weathered face grimly. Hardy Graham opened his eyes.

"Damned back-shootin' scum," he croaked. Blood spilled down his lips. Blake propped his back against the fence. Blood trickled from Graham's mouth.

"Quiet now," Blake said.

"Quiet?" came the hoarse whisper from the old man. "Who the hell wants to be quiet? Got to get him." He squinted his eyes and then winced with pain. His hand fastened on Blake's wrist. "That you, Durant?"

"Yeah."

Joy dropped to her knees at her grandfather's side and Alec Graham moved beside Durant, asking, "What happened?"

Blake shook his head. "The only thing we can be sure of is that your father needs a sawbones."

Joy pushed in closer, tears running down her face. She knelt there, shaking her head desperately while old Hardy's pained look swept from one face to the other. Men had bunched up in a half circle, all standing grimly silent.

"Pa?" Sheriff Graham said huskily. When his father's gaze settled on him, he said, "Who was it?"

"Who, boy?" the old man croaked, then he swore violently, causing Joy to jerk back, shocked. "Kane Semole, that's goddamned who. Came ridin' in like he owned the town. I was in the yard—saw him plain and got my gun. Never been the man to let scum high-ride in my territory. Never even let Custer point the way to a fight without I had my say about it. Been times in my life when blood flowed thick as packed up rain in a flooded street. Waded through it. Did what I had to."

"He shouldn't talk," Blake Durant put in. Then, as Joy made to tear a strip from her blouse, Durant pulled his yellow bandanna from around his neck and handed it to her. Joy used the bandanna to dry her grandfather's brow and then to wipe blood from his chin and lips.

"Somebody get the doc," Durant said and stood up, looking at the crowd. Tonkin immediately broke into an awkward run down the street. But old Hardy Graham shifted under his granddaughter's restraining grip and coughed blood that stained Joy's blouse. She didn't seem to notice.

"Damned scum, high-struttin' his way—had to be taken down a peg. Saw him plain and got my gun," old Hardy mumbled on, paying no attention to Joy's attempts to quieten him. "Got us a good town, boy—needs trimmin' some but between us we can do it. Kane Semole, is it? We'll see about that brat and his mean ways."

Tears flowed unchecked down Joy's cheeks. The sheriff knelt and grasped his father's hand, then bit fiercely on his bottom lip, breaking the skin and drawing blood.

"You sure, Pa?" he asked. "It was Kane Semole?"

"It was Semole," said a tall old-timer in the crowd. "Hardy was in his yard, like he said, and Kane Semole came ridin' down the street. I

102

heard Hardy speak to him and saw Semole go for his gun. Hardy never even got his rifle to his shoulder before Semole put a bullet in him. Then he was ridin' off when Hardy showed his guts and got up. Semole turned about in the saddle, his face as mean as a rattler's, and then he sent another bullet into Hardy."

Joy broke into a fit of sobbing as Hardy Graham's grip on her wrist loosened. Alec leaned forward urgently, pressing his ear against his father's moving lips. Durant saw the sheriff's face go white. Then, with a last effort, Hardy Graham croaked, "I'll get him next time, boy, you'll see. Fought my way up the Platte—shot a hundred Injuns—stood before a hangin' mob and told 'em to fry. You figure a wet-eared, dog-chewed brat like Kane … Kane Semole … could … could …"

The old man coughed up blood again and then his body jerked. His chest gave one mighty heave and fell.

Alec Graham called out, "Pa! Pa!"

Joy pressed her face against her grandfather's chest and sobbed. The men in the crowd, grim-faced and silent, shuffled their feet and shook their heads. At the back of the crowd Dobie Martin stood on his own, a twisted smile on his bruised face. Blake caught his eye and saw the sneer on the cowpuncher's lips. A quick rise of anger lifted inside Blake and Martin, seeing his face tighten, moved off.

"Therese!"

Therese Semole, having heard the shooting downtown, had locked the back door of the house. Then, picking up a shawl, she'd walked onto the front porch. When she saw the crowd gather a chill went through her. She'd seen a lot of killing, thanks to her brothers, and she knew from the attitude of the crowd that someone had been shot.

Afraid for herself, she remained there in the dark, wondering what it was all about and hoping that nobody would come her way. She had seen no movement at all, so the voice from the side of the porch shocked her.

"It's me, Kane."

Therese let out a gasp as Kane's tall figure loomed up in the darkness at the side of the house. Therese turned again and looked anxiously at the gathering of men outside the Graham house.

"Kane, did you … was it you who—?"

"Old fool pulled a gun on me," came his terse reply, then Kane Semole emerged from the darkness and stood before her, hands clamped on his lean hips. Even in the dimness she could see the hatred in his eyes.

"Who was it you shot?" she asked.

"That stupid, lyin' old Injun fighter."

"Mr. Graham?"

"Yeah. Time somebody stopped his fool talk anyway." Therese stepped back hastily as her brother came towards her, bringing an angry glint to Kane Semole's narrowed eyes.

"Somethin' wrong with you, sister?" he asked gruffly. Therese tried to hold back the tears already welling in her eyes. "He was a harmless old man, Kane, a poor old man who—"

"A damned, interfering lyin' old jasper who pulled a gun on me!" Kane Semole snorted. "Are you takin' his part and not mine?"

Therese backed to the edge of the porch and sagged against the rail. She turned her gaze from Kane's face and looked down the street. In the light of a hand-held lantern she saw Joy Graham being helped away from the fence by her father. Then she saw Dobie Martin hurrying into the shadows.

Kane spat over the rail. "Damn the luck! Maybe I was seen. We'd better get away from here so you can bring me up to date on this Blake Durant jasper and what happened to Nico."

Therese turned to him suddenly. "No! Kane, you've got to ride out. You have to get away from here. They'll come for you now. They'll hang you."

"They can come, Therese," Kane said thinly. "The whole yeller bunch of 'em can come. But you and me—now we got to go someplace where we can talk. If I was seen, they'll call here first and I ain't ready for 'em yet, not till I'm sure about what happened and I know some more about this Durant hombre."

Therese let out a cry when her brother's strong hand gripped her forearm. She tried to draw away but he exerted pressure and then shook her roughly.

"What the hell is this?" he barked. "Nico's dead, ain't he?"

"Yes, he's dead, Kane."

"Then that's what we got to think about— that's what we got to settle with this town for. Get a hold of yourself, girl. I killed an old goat who asked for it, that's all. Now let's get to the back street."

Kane jerked his sister off the porch and then he pushed her through the yard, towards a short lane leading into the darkness of the back street. Therese hesitated as soon as she regained her balance, but hearing Kane coming up fast

106

behind her, she went on, trying to compose herself, angry at herself because she had made her brother even more upset. Hardy Graham didn't really matter to her and another killing of her brother's shouldn't have unduly bothered her either. There had been so much of that in her life.

Kane pulled her to a halt in the dimness of the back street and cocked his ear, listening to the sounds from the main street. When the sounds died and peace came back into the night, he said:

"Now, about Nico. How did it happen?"

"He ran a buckboard into a stranger's horse, Kane. The stranger beat him up for it."

"Beat Nico up? Big feller?"

"Big enough, Kane. Then Nico called him in the saloon and the stranger shot him down."

Kane's face tightened with disbelief. "He got the drop on Nico, eh? Tricked him. Is that how it was, Therese?" Kane touched his gun butt and his neck muscles went tight as he clamped his teeth together.

"No, Kane," Therese said quietly. "It was a fair fight. There were twenty or so witnesses. Some of our own friends were there. They all said the same—Blake Durant killed Nico fairly."

"That's a damned lie! It's gotta be a lie!" Kane cried. "Nico was near as fast as me and that'd give him the edge on any driftin' cowpoke passin' through."

Therese shook her head emphatically. "No, Kane. You've got to listen to me. I checked. I was so angry I sent off the message to you, knowing you'd want to know and knowing you'd come back and take care of this man. But, Kane," and here her voice dropped and she studied him fearfully, "Kane, it's like I just said. Nico asked for what he got and this stranger, Blake Durant, had no grudge against him. He was forced into it."

Kane grabbed her shoulders and shook her roughly. "What the hell are you sayin', Therese? Durant killed Nico, didn't he? What else is there for us to know? Now you tell me about him. Maybe he is pretty fast. Maybe I got to take some special care with him."

"He doesn't deserve to die," Therese said. "He's a ... well, he's not like all the others. He's a good man and—"

Kane struck her on the cheek and sent her crashing to the ground. He stepped up to her before she could rise, dragged her to her feet by the hair and barked into her face, "What the hell, girl? You backin' up your brother's killer?" Therese could still feel the sting of his slap on her cheek and tears welled in her eyes again. But she defied his anger by stating firmly, "Kane, I'm telling you how it was. Don't go after him. Don't kill him. He saved me from Dobie Martin. He beat Martin down for trying to molest me. He's that kind of man, a good man, straight and fair and—"

Kane struck her again and this time Therese went sprawling on her face. She struggled to her feet and then threw herself at her brother, fingers clawing for his eyes. But Kane Semole grabbed her arms and pinned them at her sides.

"Is it you and him?" he demanded to know. "Did you take up with Durant, the man who killed Nico? Is that it, damn you, woman?"

Therese stiffened in his grip and shook her head. "No, Kane, don't say that. It's just that Mr. Durant—"

Kane shook her so violently that Therese almost lost consciousness. "Mister, is it?" He hurled her back into the laneway, then he checked his gun. As he dropped the gun back in its holster he saw a group of men moving away from his sister's house. He waited for them to go down the main street before he turned to Therese and snapped, "You stay home. I'll find Durant on my own and settle with him. Then, by hell, I'll come back for you and get you straightened out."

Therese staggered on, feeling pain through her whole body. She didn't doubt for a moment that Kane would kill Blake Durant. No man alive had the ability to stop her brother when he was on the killing trail. And he was on that now, by dint of his brush with Hardy Graham and his hatred of Durant. When she moved back onto the porch, she tried one last appeal to her brother.

"Kane, have I ever lied to you? Have I?"

Kane stood at the bottom of the steps glaring towards the town. He didn't answer.

"I never have, Kane, and you know it. Nico asked for what he got. He thought he was better than he was and he got killed finding out he was wrong. Then Dobie Martin tried to molest me and Durant stopped him. I talked to Mr. Durant after that and begged him to leave town."

"He wouldn't, eh?" Kane said. "Figures he can take me, too?"

"No, Kane. His horse is lame. He bears you no grudge and he doesn't want to fight with you. Please listen to me. There doesn't have to be any more killing. Kane, we can ride out now, right away. There are new towns opening up. We can—"

"Durant first," Kane said grimly and turned to study her. "That's what I came here for. When that's done, we'll see. I'm sorry I had to hit you, sis. Never wanted to do that."

Therese went back to the edge of the porch. "It's wrong, Kane. I can't tell you any more than that."

"Then keep quiet and wait here. If they come to you, you ain't seen me. I got to have time to check things out now, on account of that old jasper drawin' on me. But come mornin', if you like, we'll be on our way. I did all my business up north. We can go south or west, whichever way you like."

With that Kane Semole moved into the darkness. He passed within twenty yards of Dobie Martin who was flattened against the wall of a store. Kane slowed, his head turning, instinct awakening him to the presence of danger. But when only the silence and the blackness answered his searching gaze, he went on into the main street and turned into the saloon laneway.

# SEVEN

# AN OLD MAN'S WORRY

Ole Manuel stood alone on the western side of the main street and watched the crowd return from the Semole house. He hadn't expected them to find Kane Semole. In Manuel's opinion, Kane was a lot better than just an out-and-out gunfighter. He had often shown Manuel signs of having plenty of commonsense, a man who in other circumstances might have made a good lawyer or even a fine lawman. But now having slain Hardy Graham, Kane Semole was going to be a real hard man to handle from now on. Whoever tackled him would eat lead.

Uncertain how he could help either Alec Graham or Blake Durant in this crisis, Manuel

stood in the darkness and watched develop-
ments in the street. The crowd walked along
the main street and headed for the saloon, Hap
Tonkin doing a heap of talking and looking
relieved at the same time. Ole Manuel did not
blame him. No sane man wanted any part of
Kane Semole in a killing mood, or in any mood
for that matter. So, when he saw the Semole girl
and her brother Kane walk to Therese's cottage,
Ole Manuel wished he was a lot younger and
a heap bolder. Here was the chance to avenge
Hardy Graham's death. But he did nothing.
Unarmed and tensed up, he was scarcely able
to think straight because of the tension that had
hold of him. To call out to somebody up the
street might only send Semole into action again.
To approach him could mean collecting a bullet
from the gunfighter.

So he waited, telling himself that at least he
had found Semole. Now he would keep an eye
on him, and he could maybe give a warning later
to those who counted, the men who would have
to tackle Semole.

It was a good five minutes later when Ole
Manuel saw Kane Semole come through the
darkness of the cottage yard. He stiffened and
flattened back against the wall of the store. It was
dark all right, but he felt as if somebody had a tar

113

torch in his face. The way Kane Semole walked stirred fresh fear in him. The man didn't actually walk, he prowled along, making no noise, his feet scarcely seeming to touch the ground. It was effortless and graceful, catlike, with every muscle of the man tuned to do its part.

Manuel wiped his face, then his heart hammered hard as he saw Kane Semole hesitate and look around. What had he heard? He wiped his brow again and the rustle of his sleeve against the wall's timber made a harsh sound that brought a gasp from him. Semole's face turned in his direction and he expected to get a bullet. But then the big man was walking again, going past him. Manuel knew what he had to do—warn Durant—but he could see no chance of getting past Kane Semole without being challenged by the big man. He'd been given an opportunity to help the town, but fear had him in its terrible grip. He could help nobody, not Alec Graham, not Durant, not anybody in this town. A grunt of self-reproach came from him.

Then, as he was turning, determined to do something, anything but stand idly there, he saw a blur of movement from the store wall across the street. Ole Manuel pressed himself back against the wall. His hands were shaking and his breath rasped harshly in his throat. He was old, weak, tired out, a skeleton of a man who amounted to nothing. He would always be nothing.

Then he recognized Dobie Martin, the big braggart of a cowpuncher who Blake Durant had cut down to size so easily that their fight had been just a joke. He remembered how Martin's desire for Therese Semole had sparked off the trouble in the first place. Now Kane Semole was up the street looking to kill, and Dobie Martin was creeping through the night, going towards the house where Therese Semole waited.

Suddenly Manuel knew with certainty that Martin was going to take out his vengeance on the Semole girl. The old man cursed under his breath. The stinkin' weasel!

Ole Manuel's hands bunched into fists and his chest swelled with anger. His fear was gone, blotted out by his hate for Dobie Martin. He could handle Martin, he was sure of that. Martin wasn't a Nico or a Kane Semole. And he was nothing at all like Blake Durant. He was an animal.

Manuel moved away from the wall and went silently down the street. He waited until Martin had turned into the cottage yard before he chanced to cross over. Then he hesitated as Martin walked slowly, warily, checking every direction before he went onto the porch. When Martin opened the front door of the house and the bleak yellow light slashed out, Manuel hurried on. The door of the cottage closed behind Martin, then a woman's scream sounded and was cut off quickly. Then came the sound of thumping against the wall—a violent banging that made the front wall of the house shake. Ole Manuel went up the steps in big strides and crossed the porch. He had the front door open when he heard the girl cry out:

"You filthy, cowardly swine!"

Ole went in, fearless now, stirred to fury and hating with every fiber of his consciousness the giant of a man attacking Therese. Martin had her by the hair with his left hand, pulling her head back while his right hand tore the blouse from her body. Ole saw greed and lust in Martin's eyes as Therese's high, full breasts were revealed.

"No! Good God, no!" Therese screamed as Martin began to force her down to the floor.

"You and me," he said. "I've been wantin' you for a long time. Been sittin' up nights just thinking about what you'd look like with nothin' on. Now, damn you, I'm gonna find out."

Therese Semole punched at his face but Dobie Martin merely tilted her body back and planted a boot on her stomach. When she cried out in pain, he struck out with a backhanded blow against the side of her head. Then, as she slumped into semi-consciousness, he ripped her skirt away and pulled at her slip. Ole Manuel stood watching in horror as the girl's ivory-skinned thighs were exposed.

"Now I'll take you," Martin said, just as Ole Manuel charged forward and hurled himself onto the big man's back. Dobie Martin, caught by surprise, let out an oath and wheeled about, sending the old man to the floor. Therese tried to get to her feet and he punched her in the head. She sank back to the floor with a moan. Then Martin saw who his attacker was and a howl of anger came out of him.

"Why, you damned old bastard!" he roared, and he hit Ole Manuel with a punch that broke his jaw and sent him reeling across the room to slam into the wall.

Martin stood there, unsure what to do for a moment. When Manuel didn't move and he saw that Therese was unconscious, Martin hurried to the front door and peered out. There was no one in the street and the town was quiet.

He wiped the sweat from his brow and struggled to control his rapid breathing. Then, turning, he crossed the room and examined the unconscious Ole Manuel. Besides the broken jaw, Manuel's head had been gashed open. Martin gave him a boot in the ribs for good measure and then bent to drag Therese to her feet. She was limp in his hands as his lustful eyes swept over her body. His breathing grew heavy as his desire for her took charge of him. Martin tore the rest of her clothes off and carried her to the divan. He put her down and Therese's head lolled to the side. She made no sound and did not move.

Kane Semole waited. A man of infinite patience where gunfighting was concerned, he was convinced that only a careful man could stay alive in the deadly business. Kane Semole had stood again the best and gunned them down. But he had always been the first to admit that some of the dead men had been as fast on the draw as he was. It was only Kane's coolness and regard for details that had helped him win out.

Blake Durant ... He didn't know the name. He had never heard it mentioned in all the wild towns he had been in. Strange. When a man was on the drift, rubbing shoulders with hellions in saloons and cattle camps, talk invariably turned to the men making a name for themselves with their guns.

So how in hell had an unknown managed to gun down Nico, his brother? Nico had been no slouch with a gun. His fault had been an over-eagerness to prove himself. In Kane's opinion,

Nico had always been too prone to walk in where a better man might hesitate and check. Nico, he had told his sister more than once, was booked for an early trail to Boothill. Kane had known he couldn't do anything about it. Which was why he had cut out on his own, preferring to find his own trouble without any help from Nico.

Now, standing in the darkness, Kane Semole was tense. He hated being in the dark; he liked to know everything there was to know about a man he had to face. Every bit of knowledge counted, helped you to stay alive.

Three cowhands emerged from the rear of the saloon and crossed the wide yard to their horses tethered in the saloon stables. Kane Semole listened to the creak of saddle leather, to the low rumble of talk. But it wasn't until the trio went past him, not seeing him, that he heard one speak distinctly.

"I don't give a damn. I'm for the peaceful life. Martin's in town and as sour-bellied as I've seen him. Kane Semole's here, too, and already he's done one killing. So for me, Durant and Graham can have this place to themselves."

"We're comin' along with you, ain't we, Duke?" said one of the others gruffly. "So shut up, eh?"

"Just speakin' my mind, Roscoe. You want to stay, don't bother tryin' to catch up with me in

119

the morning—I'll be too far out on the prairie with the rest of the boys and the cattle."

They went on, their words fading. Kane Semole stayed where he was. He knew Dobie Martin slightly. He was a big man, slovenly in his ways, afraid of his own shadow. Once Martin had wanted to link up with him. Kane Semole sneered into the darkness. He'd have to be mighty loco to let Dobie Martin be his trail partner. Martin was a nothing.

The departing cowhand had said that Durant and Graham could have the town to themselves. Semole swore. It looked as though Durant and the lawman had joined forces. He would have to be doubly sure of his ground now. He hated lawmen but he was sensible enough to realize that people were apt to support a man wearing a badge. He would have to push Graham out of the way, keep him cowed rather than cut him down. Then he could take Durant as easy as he liked and hit the trail with no fear of the whole town coming after him.

Semole drew his gun and checked it for the third time since he'd entered the yard. There was hardly any noise from the saloon. Why? The yard in the back was too well lit for him to go to a window and check out the place.

Kane felt his patience beginning to give out. He couldn't stay here all night. Sooner or later he'd have to make his move. But he had to know exactly what kind of man Durant was, and he had to know what Alec Graham was up to.

It might even be that Alec Graham, with his father cut dawn, had found some guts.

Kane Semole cursed at himself. What the hell was he doing waiting here? To hell with Graham and to hell with Durant! He'd get this business settled right away and then he'd clear out of town. He'd take Therese along with him to look after him. He had a strong yen for some home comforts for a change after his recent hardships and the stink and dust and heat of the cattle camps. He wanted a porch with a chair on it, a cool wind in his face and a bottle within reach.

Kane Semole pushed himself away from the fence, angry at himself for his too-cautious approach to this business. A damned driftin' cowpoke! He gave a hoarse laugh and walked towards the saloon's back door. But then, when he was no more than ten feet away, with the saloon window throwing a yellow rectangle on the ground in front of him, Hap Tonkin stepped through the doorway. The saloonkeeper had a Stetson in his hand. One of the three cowhands had been hatless, Kane remembered as he dropped a hand to his gun butt.

Tonkin, looking into the yard beyond Kane Semole. gave a grunt and then he tossed the old range hat into the yard. Then, turning, he sighted the tall figure in the shadows. Suddenly his face went taut and his mouth gaped.

Kane Semole said, "Keep comin', Tonkin. Close the door after you."

Tonkin gulped. "Kane! Hell, I—"

"No talk, mister. Just close the door and walk to me. I mean you no harm."

Tonkin shuffled his feet and shifted his gaze about, then he gave a long sigh. He knew enough about Kane Semole to realize that a wrong move at this time would light the short fuse of his violence.

"Sure, Kane, sure," he mumbled and he fumbled with the knob before he got a grip on it and pulled the door closed behind him. "Hell, Kane, you've got no quarrel with me. I never did anything to—"

"I'll do the talking," Kane Semole said. "You just answer my questions."

Kane grabbed him and pulled him down the few steps.

Tonkin's face was pale and his lips were compressed. He could hardly swallow.

Semole pushed Tonkin back against the wall of the saloon and asked, "Is Durant inside?"

Tonkin nodded.

"Where exactly? How can I tell which one is him?"

"He's … he's on his own, this end of the counter, drinkin' slow, keepin' to himself."

"Is he waitin' for me?"

"Everybody figures that since you're in town, you'll go after Durant. Hell, Kane, I never once in my life did anything to you to make you—"

"Shut up, damn you!" Kane Semole released him and backed away a step. "Describe him."

Tonkin wiped sweat from his face and licked at his lips. "He's a tall man, real big and wide. Stands straight. Wears a hide coat in good order. You can't miss him, Kane. He's alone. Everybody is keeping their distance, knowin' you're about."

"And the lawman?"

Hap Tonkin shook his head. "He was in but he left. His daughter is cut up bad over the old man's death."

"Fine, Hap," Kane Semole said with a grin that brought relief to the barkeep's face. "You've helped plenty. But then you always was a helpful gent, even though maybe it was only because you was so scared of me and Nico. Now tell me about Nico and how he got it."

Now Tonkin was breathing fast again and his hands were shaking. He didn't like it when Kane Semole pretended to be affable. Pleasantness in Kane Semole was always a prelude to big trouble.

Tonkin said, "Nico called Durant inside last night. Durant killed him fair. He's good, Kane, by hell, he's real good."

"So they tell me," Kane said sourly, then he lifted his gun almost casually and slammed the butt across Hap Tonkin's head. He watched Tonkin fall to the ground, then he stepped towards the door. He tensed himself, turned the knob and entered the saloon. Closing the door behind him, his dark gaze moved along the bar and settled on the loner standing at the end of the bar counter. The rest of the customers were a long way up the room, closely bunched, sticking together. Nobody looked Kane's way as he walked deeper into the room, his footsteps loud in the silence.

"Durant!"

Blake Durant's hand froze on the edge of his glass. His mind had been a long way off in the country where he had been raised. There had been the faces of many people in his mind— his brother, boyish, eager, maturing with love for work and play in equal doses. And there had been Louise Yerby, tall and slender and warm.

Durant turned and looked at the tall man in black who stood with his feet planted wide, a hand clamped on the butt of his gun. Blake's first impression was that the stranger was a trifle worried, unsure of himself. Then he saw the lips curl and hate entered the black eyes.

Blake said, "Semole?"

"That's who I am, drifter. I came for you. I guess you know that."

"It doesn't have to be," Blake said.

Semole's glance flashed past Durant and he quickly took in the rest of the crowd. He said, "If any of you buy in, I'll shoot your guts out along with Durant's. That's a promise."

Blake moved and wiped his right hand down his shirt front. Then he elbowed back the right flap of his range coat as he measured Kane Semole with calm eyes.

"I'll say it again, Semole. It doesn't have to be. Your brother asked for all he got."

"He may have, Durant. But no matter … it's me askin' now, not him. Come away from the bar counter. Move slow and watch where you put your hand. I can take you easy and I'll do it fair, but so help me, if you try to get the jump on me I'll blast you down cold."

"I'll be careful," Blake told him coolly. "But I'm watching. You see, I can't trust any man who blasted down an old man on his last legs."

Kane Semole's face twisted. "He asked for it, damn you! That old fool Graham always asked for it—shootin' off his stupid mouth every time I saw him. He drew on me."

"We have only your word for it," Blake said. He shifted slowly away from the counter, keeping his hand away from his gun butt. None of the others in the room moved until Durant had taken a position clear of the bar. Then they began to edge away from the line of fire.

Semole stood still, his jaw working and his narrowed stare not moving from Durant. The drifter's coolness appeared to worry him a little. He had taken Nico. So he was fast, damned fast. But was he fast enough? Kane Semole didn't know.

Then the batwings burst open and Alec Graham strode into the room, gun in hand. The doors were still creaking when Semole's gaze slashed the sheriff's way. Semole's left shoulder dropped.

"Stay put, lawman," he growled.

Alec Graham stopped in his tracks and his face went white with anger. Somehow Blake knew that Alec Graham's fear was gone. Now Alec Graham had no fear for anyone. The death of his father had worked a miracle. He came straight along the bar, his gun level.

"You killed my father," he said to Kane Semole.

"Sure, lawman, because he asked for it. I done no wrong by anybody in this town and that old fool took a rifle to me. You figure I should let a pride-bloated old man cut me down for no reason at all?"

"Pa had his reasons," Alec Graham said. "And I've got mine."

Kane Semole's lips curled back in a sneer. "You have, have you, lawman? Well, there's another mistake you've made. Seems your whole life is one big line of mistakes, the first one bein' that you let yourself get born. The second mistake was when you pinned on a badge. You're gutless, lawman, right down to the heels of your boots. So git while you got the chance and keep to hell outa my hair."

"I'm holding you for trial, Semole," Alec Graham said, moving towards him. The crowd shuffled back, deathly silent. Kane Semole tilted his head to one side and his dark eyes narrowed to slits.

Then Semole said, "Keep outa this, Durant. I'll get to you later. But for now—"

His words were cut off by the explosion of a gun. Alec Graham's bullet ripped close to

Semole's head, making him jerk to the side. Then Semole's gun cleared leather and bucked in his hand. At the roar of the second shot, Alec Graham staggered back, a hole in his shoulder. Blake Durant let out a curse and dropped his hand. But as Alec Graham went down, Kane Semole turned his gun to cover Durant.

"Like I said before, Durant, make your mistake and die. You're gonna die anyway, but I'd rather gun you down fair and square so I won't have the whole fool town on my neck when I cut out. Get that gun hand up now. Up!"

Blake delayed only a split second before his fingers uncurled from his gun. Through the corner of his eye he saw Alec Graham writhing in pain on the floor.

"Make your call any time, Semole," he said.

But Kane Semole kept his gun out. He saw Graham trying to rise and he put a bullet in his wrist. The lawman's gun was jolted away and went slithering across the sawdusted boards to crash into the foot rail against the counter. Blake stiffened and deep anger took hold of him. But Semole had him pinned. He knew then that he would have to kill Kane Semole.

# EIGHT

## THE GUTLESS BREED

Ole Manuel lifted himself painfully from the floor and held his head in his hands. But the effort of rising sent a deep drive of pain into his ribs. He buckled over, groaning. For a long time he leaned against the wall, trying to clear his mind, seeing the walls of the cottage as a shapeless blur before him.

There was no sound but the swish of the wind through the doorway behind him. Ole gritted his teeth, then moaned as fresh pain worked through him. He stood there, one hand to his head and the other against his ribs. He leaned against the wall, afraid that his legs would buckle under him.

It took a few minutes before he could breathe enough air into his tortured lungs. The haze lifted before his eyes and the walls of the room took shape. He let his gaze sweep the room slowly as he tried to remember.

Then he saw Therese Semole's naked body on the divan. Her hair hung down across her face and blood stained her bosom and stomach. Ole gasped in shock and his own pain immediately left him. He shuffled across to the girl, knelt beside her and felt for a pulse. There was none. He stood there, unable to believe that this young and beautiful woman was dead.

He looked about him, his mind in a turmoil. Slowly the memory of what had happened came back to him: Kane Semole and his sister returning to their cottage after the fruitless search by the townsmen and Alec Graham ... Kane Semole walking past him, a man on edge, wary, bent on killing ... Dobie Martin leaving the shadowed doorway of the store ...

Dobie Martin!

Ole Manuel dropped beside the naked body and frantically searched for some sign of life. He couldn't leave without being sure. He saw her bruised face. Her ravaged body was already beginning to go stiff in death.

How long ago? Ole Manuel sought desperately for the answer but he couldn't be sure. He hurried to the front door and looked out. The street lights were still on. Light from the saloon fell on horses lined along the hitch rails. So business was still going on in Hap Tonkin's place.

Ole returned to the girl and placed a blanket over her body. He couldn't think of anything else he could do for her. Mopping sweat from his face and remembering his foolish attack on Dobie Martin, he swore violently. Then he stumbled off, wanting to get out of this place. Nobody would accuse him of trifling with the girl. Ole was too old, was past all that. And they would believe his story about Martin, because Martin had shown his hand before in this regard. The town would hang Dobie Martin and Ole Manuel would be there to witness the last kicks of the swine.

He was halfway across the yard when the first shot came. Ole stopped. The darkness was a blanket of quiet about him. A second shot sounded, then came a deeper silence.

Ole pulled at his shirt collar, feeling he was choking. Where was Dobie Martin? Where was Kane Semole? The girl was dead. Who had fired off those shots? Was Durant dead?

Blake Durant! Ole licked at his dry lips. Ole had tended the loner's horse and done a good job on the animal. Durant had not been angry with him, just a trifle resentful that he had interfered. Well, Manuel knew he'd helped some in keeping Durant in this town, and he'd done that for a very good reason. Durant could take Kane Semole, Ole was positive of it. With Kane Semole dead, Alec Graham could run a clean and peaceful town again. But there would still be the rapist-killer, Dobie Martin.

Ole Manuel broke into a shambling run. He cut into the main street and headed for the saloon. He was within fifteen yards of the batwings when he saw Dobie Martin pressed against the outside wall, gun in hand, peering in through the window. Ole didn't stop. Gunless, he was powerless to do anything about Dobie Martin. But there were men in this town who could.

Ole hurled himself into the saloon through the batwings and saw Blake Durant and Kane Semole facing each other, waiting, both intent on the fight to come. He also saw, in a quick glance, Alec Graham lying on the floor at the feet of some twenty silent, grim-faced men.

Ole skidded to a halt, then worked his way to the bar counter. "Hold it!" he called out and pointed to the window. "Martin's there. He raped and murdered your sister, Semole."

Kane Semole, leaning slightly forward, his body bunched and tensed for action, threw a hot glance Manuel's way. "What's that, old man?"

"Just left your house, Semole. Your sister's there, dead and mauled. I saw Dobie Martin do it—and he's outside now."

Kane Semole's face went black with rage. "You're lyin' just like the rest of this town! You all want me to leave Durant alone. That's all you want!"

"No!" Ole Manuel cried. "See for yourself. There!"

He pointed and at that moment the window glass exploded. A gun barked four times. Blake Durant felt one of the bullets tug at the shoulder of his coat. A second ripped skin from his neck. He swung about, forgetting all about Kane Semole. He believed Ole Manuel unconditionally. The old man had no cause to lie.

Kane Semole let out a grunt and his gun bucked. Then a bullet slammed into his chest and sent him reeling. A second slug blasted his spine as he still staggered under the impact of the first bullet. A loud cry of pain came from him.

Blake Durant went forward in long strides. When he reached the boardwalk, a horse was running down the street. The rider was flattened on the neck of the animal and his spurs jabbed viciously. Blake emptied his gun after the fleeing rider but had no idea if his shots hit home. The horse went on, pounding into a side street, headed for the grassed prairie beyond the town.

Blake Durant moved quickly to the horses tied at the hitch rail. He had already freed one when Ole Manuel hurried out to him.

"No, Durant! No sense going after him now. Morning will be soon enough. Country's soft. You'll pick up his trail easy in daylight."

Blake turned to the old man, a thoughtful look on his face.

"Anyway, you're wanted inside," Manuel said. "Semole's got the whole crowd pinned down. He's hurt bad, so bad he don't know what he's doing. I tell you, he's loco. He'll kill everybody."

Blake looked towards the batwings. He eased Manuel aside, telling him to stay back, then he breasted the swing doors apart. When he stood inside, empty gun in hand, he saw Kane Semole propped against the far wall, his gun leveled on him.

Blake walked slowly towards him.

Kane Semole lifted his Colt a fraction. His shirt was a mess of blood and his face was white with pain. Blake stopped a short distance from him and said:

"What Manuel said about your sister was right. Martin proved that by shooting and then running."

Kane Semole went on studying Blake sullenly. "Who knows for sure?" he grated.

"I believe him, and I think you do, too. This other business doesn't have to go on. You need a sawbones."

"I'm past that, Durant," Kane Semole said. He prodded two bullets from his gunbelt and pushed them into his gun cylinder. Kane tried to push himself to his feet but didn't have the strength.

Then he said, "You still gonna answer my call, Durant? You got the guts for that?"

"I've got the guts, Semole, but you're no match for me now, not hurt as bad as you are. Your arm's gone numb."

Kane Semole swore through his teeth, but he clamped his left hand under his right wrist and held the gun steady.

"I'm a match for a tinhorn like you any time, day or night, Durant. You reckon you killed Nico

135

fair. All right, prove it. Back up and let somebody help me to my feet."

"Meantime I'll load my gun, Semole," Blake said easily. "I emptied it shooting at Martin as you must have heard."

Kane Semole squinted painfully at him and drew in his breath. "Fair enough," he said, and most of the hate had gone from his voice. Blake dug bullets out of his belt and began filling his gun. As he did, two men left the bar counter and helped Kane Semole to his feet.

When he was upright, Semole shoved them away roughly, saying, "Okay, all of you keep back now. This is between me and Durant. You'll see, all of you, whether I'm guilty of back-shootin' an interfering old fool. I'll get Durant here where you can all see. Then I'm headin' out after Dobie Martin."

Blake put up his gun. The action brought a scowl to Kane Semole's face. Then he holstered his own gun and steadied himself against the wall, hands slack at his sides. His face was gleaming with sweat and his lips were pressed so tightly together they looked like a scar across his face. His cheeks had gone sallow and his breathing was tortured.

Blake said, "You're in no condition for this, Semole. I don't want it this way. In a day or two, when you're in better shape I'll still be about. I'll stay and I'll make you answer for killing old Hardy Graham."

Kane Semole's lips peeled back, showing strong white teeth. "We'll see, big man." Then his right hand dropped. But when the fingers clamped on the gun butt, he couldn't take a firm hold.

He was still fumbling when his body pitched forward. He let out a curse and reached out for something to hang onto, to keep himself upright. But there was nothing in front of him. He hit the floor on his face and a loud explosion of breath came from him. When he didn't move, Blake Durant walked slowly towards him. He could see the gaping hole in Semole's back and the whole of the shirt and the top of his Levis were soaked with the gunfighter's blood. A gasp came from almost every man in the room.

Ole Manuel, who had come in despite Durant's advice, choked, "My God, look at his back!"

His words were not needed. Every man in that room was looking at Kane Semole's back, seeing the hole, wondering how the man had stayed on his feet for so long.

Then Blake Durant lifted Semole from the floor and turned him over. He stared into the glazed eyes of the gunfighter. He carried him to the wall and propped him there.

Kane Semole coughed up blood and croaked, "Would've taken you, Durant. Damn you, you know it!"

"Maybe," Blake said.

"Would have, damn you! No stinkin' polecat drifter like you could ever …" Kane Semole's body shook under a spasm of coughing and Blake held him against the wall. When he stopped coughing Kane Semole sat hunched over. Life was fast leaving his body.

"Get Manuel," he breathed hoarsely.

Manuel, hearing him, came forward and dropped beside him. Kane grasped Manuel's wrist, pulled him closer and said, "You sure about that Martin jasper, Manuel?"

"I'm sure, Mr. Semole."

"Mister?" Kane Semole said back and a tight smile played along the edge of his mouth. "You hear that, Durant? He called me mister. First time."

"Deservedly," Durant said.

Kane Semole's eyes closed against the pain and his breathing was fast and labored. "What's that you said, Durant?"

"Nobody will ever know who would have won between us," Blake said. "But everybody will remember that you had chances to gun me down and held off. So you're not a murderer."

Kane Semole looked past Durant's shoulder at the unmoving crowd of tense-featured, silent men.

"That so, eh, Durant?"

"It's so, Semole."

Kane Semole grinned, then he breathed in deeply again and gripped Manuel's wrist harder. "You saw Martin maul my sister and kill her? No mistake?"

Ole Manuel nodded. "I was there and I tried to stop him. He hit me, busted my jaw like you can see, beat in one of my ribs."

Kane looked intently at the old jailer and after a time he nodded. "I'm obliged, old man, real obliged." Then he held Durant's stare for a moment and worked his neck as if freeing a cramp from it. Cold sweat ran down his face.

"Durant—my sister, Therese—she told me about you. Said you was all right. She had a feeling for you. I couldn't understand that. All I knew was you killed my brother, so I'd've killed you."

Blake just nodded.

"Martin, you get him, eh? You get him for Therese and for me. Shoot his stinkin' guts out and then leave him for the buzzards to tear apart. Will you do that?"

Blake Durant held Kane Semole's stare. He'd already made up his mind what he would do to Dobie Martin. Kane Semole's request meant nothing to him.

But he said, "You know I will, Semole."

Kane Semole grinned tightly. "Yeah, I know. Funny, Durant, you and me … different circumstances, maybe we would have got along together … had some laughs even."

Blake felt Kane's Semole's body go limp. When he looked at the gunfighter's face, he saw the smile fading from his lips as death came. Then Kane Semole toppled forward and Blake eased him down.

Standing, Blake looked about the barroom. Hap Tonkin, blood streaming down the side of his face, staggered in from the yard. He stopped when he saw Durant and the body of Kane Semole.

Tonkin glared at Kane Semole's body and grunted a curse. Then, "You got him, eh, Durant? Damned fine. Real damn fine."

Blake ignored him and crossed to where Alec Graham lay. He checked the lawman's wounds and told Tonkin to take care of him, then he walked along the bar slowly. Once more he was a man alone. He went into the main street and saw Joy Graham on her porch, her face grey with strain.

Blake crossed the street, stood at the fence and said, "Your father's been hurt, but not too badly. He needs you."

Joy ran down the steps and across the yard without waiting to hear more. But when she reached the boardwalk she hesitated, then turned.

"You're hurt," she said.

Blake felt his wound, found his shirt sticky with blood. But the bleeding had all but stopped. "I'll be all right."

Joy said, "Go into the house, Mr. Durant. You'll find everything you want in the back room. I'll get back as soon as I can."

Blake watched her go, then he opened the gate into the yard. He turned on the porch and saw her rushing into the saloon. The street was deserted and quiet. Blake took off his range coat, opened the door of the house and went in. On the table in the front room was his yellow bandanna, folded carefully, still damp. He picked it up and looked down thoughtfully at it. Louise Yerby. Joy Graham. They had so much in common.

Blake moved to the back of the house, took off his shirt and washed the blood from his neck. The wound was no more than a graze. He tied the bandanna about it and walked to the chair in the corner of the room. From that position he could see out into the back yard beyond which were the foothills and the trails leading in every direction across this wild frontier. Trails that led nowhere as far as he was concerned.

He relaxed, closed his eyes. Tomorrow at first light, he would go after Dobie Martin. He'd find Martin and he'd settle with him for what he had done to the girl and to Kane Semole. Then he would be free to pick up his life again.

He smiled without humor when he realized how little time had passed since he rode down the main street and came into conflict with Nico Semole. Nico was dead. So were Hardy Graham, Therese and Kane Semole. Alec Graham was badly wounded and Ole Manuel had a broken jaw and perhaps some broken ribs.

But Dobie Martin lived. For the time being.

Blake Durant didn't hear Joy Graham come in half an hour later. Nor did he stir when she put a blanket across his knees and worked a pillow behind his head. He didn't know either that she stood before him, her face grave with worry, her heart full of sadness, yet with a curiosity about him which eased some of the deep worry away. He slept on, and Joy Graham, having been assured that her father would pull through under the doctor's care, went to her room, undressed and lay awake on the bed, still thinking about this strange man, this loner, who had so recently come into her life, but who had already left a mark which she knew time would not be able to obliterate.

# NINE

# TRAIL OUT

Ole Manuel had swept out the jailhouse, one of his daily chores, and now he stood on the boardwalk, looking at the town in which so much trouble had occurred. It was a good town, he told himself, despite everything. A pity old Hardy Graham was dead, but Ole decided it was perhaps better for Alec Graham that he was. Alec could now think for himself, and Ole Manuel considered that the sheriff had enough grey matter to be able to make a good job of it.

He gave the boardwalk a last casual swipe with his old broom and was turning to go inside when he saw Blake Durant come down the street on his black stallion. The horse looked in fine fettle, and his action was not in the least proppy.

Manuel stood the broom against the jailhouse wall and walked to the edge of the boards. Durant stopped short of the old man, keeping the sun across his shoulders, his long shadow falling across Manuel.

"Where would you look for Martin, old man?" Blake asked. There was no hint of tension in his face and his voice was as calm as Manuel had ever heard it. But then, after a moment's consideration, he decided he had never really seen Durant excited at all, not even when Nico Semole had come for him.

"Due west. Martin's been around these parts for a long time and is known in just about every town. But he ain't known west of here."

"Does he have any close friends?"

Manuel shrugged. "He rode with some hands on the place he worked. They'd come to town together and get drunk more often than not, play cards, fun it up some. Hard to say with a bunch like that who's a friend and who's just along for the ride."

"He wouldn't call on those friends, eh?" Blake asked.

Ole Manuel thought about the question for a moment. Then he shrugged again. "He's desperate, scared out of his boots. He knows he missed you when he had the chance, and I guess he knows you'll hunt him down, especially after what he did to the girl."

Blake Durant looked westward. "Tell Graham I've gone on," he said, then he let the big horse have its head.

Manuel called after him, "Watch him close, Durant. Martin's a back-shooter for sure. He won't let you get close to him if he can help it."

"Bury Kane Semole well," Blake returned and slapped Sundown on the right shoulder. The big black responded vigorously and pounded his way out of town.

Ole Manuel stood in the street now, hat pushed back, his hand-me-down clothes flapping under the shift of a stiff breeze. He grinned, feeling pleased with himself. For an old man he had come out of this troublesome business real well. He watched until Durant was no more than a speck in the distance before he turned back into the jailhouse. Alec Graham was sitting up on his cell bunk. "Was that Durant?"

"Yes. Gone after Martin," Manuel told him.

Graham tried to rise but a drive of pain made him wince and remain still.

"Way I see it, that's exactly how it should be," Manuel said, sweeping at the jailhouse floor.

"Wouldn't like to be in Dobie Martin's boots right now. Reckon he'll find out that this frontier is no bigger'n a horse yard when a man like Durant is on his trail."

Manuel went out to the back, leaving Alec Graham scowling after him.

Lee Scanlon recognized Durant as he came up the ranch house clearing. Blake looked towards the two cowhands still saddling their horses. Neither made any comment.

Scanlon muttered, "Stay back. I'll see what he wants."

He rode down the clearing and stopped short of Durant halfway down. Blake eyed him calmly.

"I want Dobie Martin," he said.

Scanlon nodded. "Figured somebody'd come. What did he do?"

Blake Durant told him. Scanlon swore and waved for the other pair to come up. He introduced them as Tom Field and Stan Pittwell, the cowhands who had left Dobie Martin when he first tried to have his way with Therese Semole.

"Durant's looking for Martin," Scanlon said. "What do you fellers reckon?"

It was Tom Field who spoke up. "Where else but straight west, Lee. Towards the river."

"Which is in flood," Scanlon said. "Had heavy rains most of this half-year. River takes a long time to drop."

Blake Durant looked that way, seeing the mountains rising in the distance. "How far?" he asked.

"Day and a half's ride," Scanlon told him. "Raped the girl, you said?"

"No doubt about that."

Scanlon looked at Field and Pittwell again, then he said, "Can you wait until we pack some grub, Durant? We feel kinda implicated. Therese Semole was maybe no angel but she didn't deserve what Dobie did, that's for sure. Be only a few minutes."

"No time," Durant said and pushed his horse past. He had only gone on a few yards when Scanlon called:

"If you don't know the country out there, Durant, you might miss him. River comes down through the gorge. In flood time a man could easily get blocked by the rapids. You got to push right on to the end of the hills before coming into it. Only that way—"

Blake Durant was listening and not showing it as he went on. When he heard a grunt from Scanlon he kicked Sundown into a run. The big black, eager to be on the trail, bounded forward powerfully. Before the three cowmen could make up their minds to follow, Durant was off the clearing and heading into the bottom country.

He rode all that day, occasionally picking up the tracks of a single horse heading west. He made only one camp during that time, at a small branch creek. The heat of the day was fierce and the humidity was high in this closed-in country. Sundown showed no signs of slowing down, pushing on in obedience to the demands of the man in the saddle. At dusk they reached rising country near a chain of hills. Blake thought he could hear an undercurrent of sound, of water flowing free and full somewhere close.

He pressed on until darkness came and he struck camp. He rested completely, his mind blotted out to all thoughts but the man ahead, a man he sensed was watching his back-trail and sweating heavily about pursuit. Martin had a night's start on him. If he reached the river first and crossed, Blake knew it would be a devil of a job to track him down in the desert country beyond the mountains. Perhaps there were settlements there and the inhabitants might give him some information. But they might be like the communities dotted along most borders, carrying people who minded their own business and said nothing to strangers.

It was an hour before sunup when Durant continued on his way. He swung wide past a tall hill. Now he could hear the rumble of water clearly. He remembered Scanlon's advice and struck away from the mountain. The country lay flat before him, treeless, rocky, empty.

Then he saw a shack in the distance. He drew rein and looked around him. He could see only one way to approach the shack without being observed. This was across a butte that sheltered a low-lying river bank. The roar of water going over rapids told him that he was close to the flooded river. A crossing there would probably be dangerous, even for a strong horse.

Blake rode down to the butte, moved through a cluster of boulders and stopped Sundown a hundred feet or so short of the shack. There was no sound from the place and no sign of a horse outside. He came out of the saddle and went forward on foot, leaving Sundown standing with the reins trailing. Reaching the rear of the shack, Blake walked carefully down its side. The door in the front was closed, and a single window flashed in the sunlight.

Blake walked to the door, braced himself, then sent the door crashing in with a well-placed kick.

The shack was deserted.

Blake gave it a brief inspection and saw where Martin had cooked a meal and used the old bunk. The smell of burning wood still hung in the room, but it meant little. Smoke scent would stay in a closed room for weeks. So he still had no idea how far in front of him Dobie Martin was.

Going back to Sundown, Blake swung into the saddle. He came back to the shack and went past it, heading for the river. The water was running fast, in one section boiling furiously over huge rocks in midstream. He went along the bank, picking up the tracks of a single horse. The tracks, he decided, were only a few hours old.

Blake pushed Sundown on at a faster gait and for the rest of the morning he rode the timbered slopes running parallel to the river. At noon he stopped at the remains of a campfire. The ashes were still warm.

He rode slower now, his eyes searching. After another hour he came to a place where the high river banks leveled out, dropping away to a flat grassy section. The tracks he followed went straight across the open stretch towards a low river bank, out from which the river narrowed and flowed peacefully.

Dobie Martin had crossed here! Blake Durant was positive of it. He was close to the killer—and getting closer because Martin's tired horse had obviously shortened stride. Then Blake heard a far-off gunshot. Blake hit Sundown into a run and paid no heed to the blasting heat of the afternoon. He rode along the low river bank and then he drove his horse into the water. He made the crossing without any difficulty, but as he was coming up the other bank, he saw a thin trail of smoke rising from under a canopy of branches. Blake swung out of the saddle, hitched Sundown to a bush and proceeded on foot. When he stopped again, he could see the huddled shape of a man sitting before a fire. A horse lay on the ground on its side yards away, unmoving. There was a bullet hole in its head. Which explained the gunshot Blake had heard.

Blake could have killed the crushed and trail-weary Dobie Martin where he sat, but instead he picked up a stout stick and hurled it away. When it crashed through brush on the other side, Dobie Martin jumped to his feet, gun in hand, his back to Blake.

Martin called, "That you, Lee? Tom? Stan?" He waited. "Damn you, who's out there?"

Dobie Martin began to back away from the fire, moving towards Blake.

"Lee, if it's you, what I said still stands. I got it all worked out. No sense in working for other folks. Better to take your own cut and to hell with the rest of 'em."

Martin kept backing away, then he tripped on a stone and swung about, his face white with fear as his gaze flicked to the left and right.

Blake knelt behind the brush and said, "Your friends wanted no part of you, Martin."

Martin swallowed hard. He held his gun so tightly that every muscle in his forearm bulged. He waved the Colt about, desperate for a sight of the man who spoke.

When he saw no one, he backed off in another direction and then suddenly he turned and broke into a run. Blake Durant took careful aim and fired. Martin's left leg whipped out from under him with the impact of the slug and he went down on his side. Only then, as Martin writhed about and tried to rise, did Blake Durant show himself.

Abject fear showed in Dobie Martin's face. Before him stood a man who had beaten him with bare fists, humbled him, and caused him to be cast out by his employer. His gun jerked up and hatred replaced the fear in his eyes.

"Damn you, Durant! Damn you to hell!"

His gun barked. A wild shot that missed badly. Blake Durant stood his ground, despising Martin, wanting him to suffer. He could visualize this animal mauling the slender Therese Semole. He could see him raining punches on her face and chest; and later …

Blake punched off four shots. The first crashed into Martin's chest, sending him rolling onto his back. The second tore the throat out of the man, and the third and fourth joined the first in his chest. Dobie Martin gave one gurgling scream and his body stiffened. The gun slipped from his hand and his head hit the ground with a dull thud.

Blake Durant didn't bother to examine the body. He brought Sundown there and heaved Dobie Martin's blood-soaked body behind the saddle. Mounting, he rode back across the river and past the mountains, then he headed for the ranch where Dobie Martin had worked.


"He raped and murdered a girl who belonged to this town," Sheriff Alec Graham told his daughter as he tightened the cinch strap on his horse in the jailhouse yard. "It's my duty to hunt him down."

"But you're not fit to ride, Pa," Joy said. "The doctor said—"

"Too many people for too long have been telling me what to do and not to do, Joy. Leave well enough alone, will you?"

Joy stepped back, shocked by the severity of his tone. But a deeper respect for her father showed in her face a moment later.

"Then I'll come along, Pa," she said.

"No! Martin's a killer!"

"Just to look after you, Pa, in case the bleeding starts again. You can't expect me to stay here in town and worry myself sick, wondering if you're bleeding to death out there."

Alec Graham grunted something under his breath. Then Ole Manuel, who'd been packing provisions into Graham's saddlebags, put in, "Can't see it would do any harm, Sheriff. That shoulder will need new dressings from time to time and it'll be a long ride now that the others have such a big start on you."

Graham looked angrily at the jailer, then he gave a grin. His shoulder did hurt like blazes.

"Okay, then, but by hell you keep out of my hair, Joy. If I say to stay put, you stay there."

"Certainly, Pa," Joy said eagerly, then she hurried off to saddle her mare.

When she and her father were riding out some fifteen minutes later, he eyed her knowingly for a while and said:

"It's more than just Dobie Martin, isn't it, girl?"

Joy felt blood flash to her face. She lowered her eyes. "What else could it be, Pa?"

155

"Durant."

Joy's mouth opened but no sound came from her.

"You're worried about him," Graham said.

She nodded.

"Figured it might be him, Joy. You were alone with him all last night, in the house. Somethin' coulda happened."

"Pa!"

Graham ignored her indignation. "Don't know rightly what to think of that jasper. He's so damn quiet and he keeps to himself most of the time. He can handle a gun and use his fists, and I guess he's made a big name for himself in my town. That kind can easily turn the heads of young women. Like with Therese Semole, for instance."

"Pa, how could you think—?" Joy began again but Graham waved her to silence and went on:

"I can think any way I like, Joy. I'm your father so that gives me the right to check on what you're up to. I guess you are worried about me, but you'd come all this way even if I wasn't hurt. And I know you ain't got nothin' special against Dobie Martin so you'd want to be on hand to see him arrested or killed. So, it's got to be Durant. Now, I want to know what the hell went on between you."

Joy was silent for a long time before she said, "Pa, nothing happened. You have my word on that. Why, Mr. Durant hardly knows I'm alive."

Graham grunted and kicked his horse on. They cut down into the bottom country, not speaking to each other, and then they approached Karl Parry's ranch house. As they did so they saw a lone rider bearing down from the high country beyond the barn. Joy stopped the mare, grabbing at her father's arm. Alec Graham reined up his horse, put field-glasses to his eyes and squinted ahead.

After a moment he muttered, "It's Durant all right."

"Is he … is he all right, Pa? Can you see clearly enough?"

Alec Graham said tonelessly, "He don't look hurt to me. Seems to be totin' somethin' back of his saddle."

"Dobie Martin," Joy said, her face brightening. "He found him, Pa. I knew he would."

Alec Graham gave a grunt. After a few minutes he saw some of Karl Parry's hands running towards the stables. Blake Durant stopped his horse short of them and pushed Dobie Martin's body to the ground. Then he backed Sundown off, wheeled him away and rode back the way he had come.

Joy cried out, "Pa, he's leaving."

"He did what he had to," Alec Graham said.

"But, Pa, why?"

"A man like him, girl, is kinda hard to understand. Durant drifted into our town, minding his own business. Nico Semole made trouble for him and he killed him. Then Kane Semole made trouble and Kane ain't gonna bother nobody no more. Then Dobie Martin …"

Graham's voice trailed off. He looked at his daughter and saw tears welling in her eyes. He kicked his horse into a run and Joy followed. When he reached the Parry bunch he found them standing around the dead man on the ground. The four bullet holes in Dobie Martin told their own story. Graham, seeing his daughter go pale, rode to her.

He said, "He never gave anything of himself to our town, girl. Or to you, as you said. So now, he's gone on his way. A loner. No other name for him. Blake Durant, a man alone, the odd man out. Ain't nobody ever gonna change that."

Tears coursed down Joy's cheeks and a stifled sob came from her. "Won't he ever come back, Pa?"

"Hard to tell with his kind."

Joy turned her horse and kicked it forward. Her father gave her a quick look but stayed where he was. Joy raced her horse past the barn and up into the beginning of the foothills.

Blake Durant had stopped Sundown half a mile ahead. He looked at her, saw her hair flowing in the breeze. Joy Graham saw him lift a hand and wave.

She let her horse walk on a pace or two and pulled on the reins. Blake Durant had not come back to her. She sat there with the sun full in her face, a chill riding her body. She did not know this man. Nobody actually knew him. He had come out of the emptiness and done what he had to do. People had crowded him and he had killed them.

Perhaps, she thought, it would always be like that. Durant, as her father had said, was a loner and wanted to be no more than that. But she whispered:

"Come back, Mr. Durant. One day, come back. You'll find me waiting for you."

Blake Durant was out of sight when she finally lowered her gaze. Joy Graham didn't know it and never would, but only minutes ago Blake Durant had fought a struggle within himself and had been on the verge of riding back. But there had been another woman, a long time ago, a woman who'd come between Joy and Blake.

So Blake Durant rode into the emptiness, feeling the familiar loneliness closing in on him. He rode slowly, thoughtful, not thinking about what might he ahead. But one day, somewhere, something would happen and he'd no longer drift. He knew it.

He rode on, a loner on a strange trail, heading nowhere.